SNAKE EYES

SNAKE EYES

A novel by
David Jacobs

Based upon the screenplay
by David Koepp
Story by Brian De Palma
and David Koepp

BERKLEY BOULEVARD BOOKS, NEW YORK

SNAKE EYES

A Berkley Boulevard Book / published by arrangement with
Viacom Consumer Products, Inc.

PRINTING HISTORY
Berkley Boulevard edition / August 1998

All rights reserved.
Copyright © 1998 by Paramount Pictures Corporation.
This book may not be reproduced in whole or in part,
by mimeograph or any other means, without permission.
For information address: The Berkley Publishing Group,
a member of Penguin Putnam Inc.,
200 Madison Avenue, New York, New York 10016.

The Penguin Putnam Inc. World Wide Web site address is
http://www.penguinputnam.com

ISBN: 0-425-16637-6

BERKLEY BOULEVARD
Berkley Boulevard Books are published by The Berkley Publishing Group,
a member of Penguin Putnam Inc.,
200 Madison Avenue, New York, New York 10016.
BERKLEY BOULEVARD and its logo are trademarks belonging to
Berkley Publishing Corporation.

PRINTED IN THE UNITED STATES OF AMERICA

10 9 8 7 6 5 4 3 2 1

ONE

A heavyweight championship boxing match is a world-class event. So is a hurricane. The two were on a collision course on a night at the start of a big Labor Day weekend in Atlantic City, New Jersey, the gambling mecca of the east. The fight was the Tyler-Ruiz title bout. The hurricane was a storm named Jezebel. As fight time neared, the storm center was still a few hours away from Atlantic City. Maybe it wouldn't hit at all, but would veer harmlessly out to sea, bypassing the area completely. That's how the power brokers were playing it, the big guys who called all the shots. The fight was still set to go.

Atlantic City is a seaside resort. Its world-famous Boardwalk runs north–south, bordering the beach. Most of the casinos are on the Boardwalk. Atlantic City Arena, where the fight was being held, is on the Boardwalk.

Rain and wind lashed the city. Visibility was poor. The streets around the arena were clogged by a massive traffic jam. There were plenty of stalled cars, too, which didn't help. Pacific Avenue, the main thoroughfare running parallel to the Boardwalk, was a mass of metal. Nothing was moving but the frustrated drivers leaning on their horns. Their protests were noisy but futile. They wouldn't be going anywhere for a long time.

Rick Santoro cruised the side streets, probing along the edges of the crush. When he had gotten as close as he could without getting jammed up himself, he pulled up beside the curb and parked his car. To hell with it, he'd walk the rest of the way.

He opened the door a crack, and the dome light came on, filling the interior of the car with yellow brightness. He was in his thirties, lean, wiry, with a long hawklike face and dark, deepset eyes. His eyes were warm and soulful, while his mouth was a hard line with a cynical twist in the corner, setting up an interesting tension in his face. He was handsome in an offbeat way, attractive to women, as long as they were smart enough not to "loan" him any money. Most of them did, anyway.

He was wearing a thin black leather coat, a lightweight sportshirt, jeans, and thick-soled, steel-toed workingman's boots.

He paused, hand on the door handle. The car shook so hard that for an instant he thought that the engine had thrown a rod; then he remembered that he had switched it off. It was the wind that was shaking the car. It shrieked through the hairline crack of the fractionally opened door, but he could barely hear it above the pounding rain.

He pushed against the door and the wind pushed back, holding it in place. He had to use some muscle to shove it open. The wind drove the rain sideways, soaking him even before he'd gotten out of the car.

He stepped into the street, the storm, and the night. He had to take a wide stance to keep from being blown off his feet. Wild! Well, at least he wouldn't have to worry about car thieves. They had too much sense to come out in this mess.

The side street ran east–west. Rick went east, walking hunched far forward, bent almost double. It was the only way he could make any progress against the wind.

Streetlamps swayed, rattling, doing crazy things to the light. Rick came to a cross-street. On the other side, the curb was lined with parked cars, stretching east toward the arena, with not a single empty space to be had.

A few more blocks, and the side street met Pacific Avenue at right angles. Traffic was gridlocked on the avenue, with hundreds of cars choking all lanes. The spaces between the bumpers could be measured in inches. It was bright, noisy chaos. Cops in rain slickers waved flashlight batons and blew whistles and screamed and cursed, barely making a dent in the mess.

East of the avenue, occupying a site the size of a city block, stood Atlantic City Arena. A huge hulking structure that looked like a cross between a fortress and a cathedral was ablaze with lights. North of and next to it was the Powell Millennium casino-hotel, a massive newly built complex. A half-dozen blocks north of that was the Showboat. South of the arena was Trump's Taj Mahal, and beyond that, Resorts. In the storm, the casinos looked like drowned wonder castles, their colored lights rainbow blurs.

The arena's main entrance was on the east face of the building, fronting the Boardwalk. Beyond the Boardwalk was a strip of beach, and then the ocean. The storming sky was black and the sea was black, and there was no telling where one began and the other ended. At the water's edge was a ruffled white fringe of surf breaking violently on the sands a stone's throw away from the Boardwalk. The beach was wider than that, but most of it was now buried under water. And the water was rising.

Rick made for the arena's front entrance, which was facing the sea. It was brutal out here in the open, with crosswinds buffeting him, trying to knock him down.

The arena was a relic of a bygone age, built long before legalized gambling had come to Atlantic City. Beside it stood the shape of the future, the Millennium casino-hotel. Parts of the new complex were still under construction, but the casino-hotel was open for business. Having a heavyweight championship fight taking place next door didn't hurt, either.

A crowd of ticket-holders was massed outside the front of the arena, trying to get in. The downpour fell on them hard and heavy, buoyed by whipping winds. The winds were rising, too.

The people-mass was bunched together, heads bowed, backs bent under the rain, shuffling forward in agonizingly slow lockstep.

To hell with that. Rick ducked the crowd, avoiding it. He struck off on a tangent, angling off to one side where the crowd wasn't. Cops and guards were keeping people out.

Rain turned the stone front stairs into miniature waterfalls, and Rick splashed through them. At the top of the stairs, a broad, flat platform fronted the row of thick glass double doors that was the main entrance. At the north end, away from the others, were a couple of single doors, closed to the general public. Rick crossed to them, passing a TV camera crew that was setting up in front of the arena's steel-framed marquee tower. Ordinarily, the sight of a TV crew would have exerted a magnetic pull on him, but tonight he had sense enough to come in out of the rain. All it took was a world title bout and a tempest.

A handful of uniformed cops in rain gear was grouped in front of the single doors. A couple of them started forward to shoo him away, then backed off when they saw who it was. They knew him. Who in Atlantic City didn't know Rick Santoro?

They passed him through, waving and grinning as he flashed them the high sign. A dozen or so stragglers on the edge of the crowd caught the play and decided that they'd get in that way, too. The cops sent them back the way they came, fast.

Rick went through one of the single glass doors, inside. He was in a carpeted entryway as big as a barn. It was good to be out of the wet. Rainwater ran off him, spattering the floor. He wiped his face with both hands, pushing the wet hair back from his forehead.

At the far end of the space was a phalanx of uniformed ticket-takers. Rick didn't have a ticket, but he was waved through anyway. They knew him.

Now he was in the lobby. It was as big as an airplane factory and as noisy, with swirling people-knots everywhere. At opposite ends of the space, the walls were hung with billboard-sized posters of the title bout contenders, Tyler and Ruiz, the champion and the challenger.

Rick looked around, starting to catch the buzz, the rush that comes from being at the center of things, where the action is. Being a player.

Rick Santoro: Mr. Inside.

•   •   •

Outside, the TV crew was doing a run-through of an introductory segment that would be going out live a few minutes later. The fight was being broadcast as a cable television pay-per-view event. Thanks to satellite-TV hookups, it would be seen by millions of subscribers worldwide—weather permitting. Right now, the weather didn't seem too cooperative.

The broadcast chores were being handled by a special Powell PPV network production team. The crew doing the outdoor remote consisted of a female announcer, a cameraman, a lighting guy, and a general assistant. That was a bigger crew than normal, but the storm was complicating everything. The assistant's main task was basically to keep the equipment from being blown away.

The announcer, Anthea, was standing in front of the tower marquee, using it as a backdrop. The marquee was an impressive steel structure, a couple of stories tall, bearing the corporate logo of Gilbert Powell Industries. Powell was the former Air Force general and hero of Operation Desert Storm who had gone into the private sector and made a megafortune as a defense contractor supplying sophisticated hardware in the aerospace industry. From there he had diversified, getting into the gaming business when his financial advisors showed him the big profits that could be made fast from legalized gambling.

Now, Powell Resorts International, the gaming division of his corporate empire, was a power in the gambling world, with extensive operations in Las Vegas, Atlantic City, and the Bahamas, and lesser sites in most states where the people had voted gambling in. Powell never had any trouble getting his casinos licensed. State gaming boards were only too happy to license this respected American hero and businessman who was free of any taint of Mob ties. He made gambling look as wholesome as Mom's apple pie.

He owned the Millennium casino-hotel and the Atlantic City Arena. The marquee tower was the symbol of his power. Its four legs were built in the shape of mock missiles, signifying the aerospace technology that was the bedrock of his vast fortune. The missile-shaped pillars were long, slim tubes of shiny steel, tapering to sharp warhead points. Atop them was an enormous steel sphere, bigger than a wrecking ball, a globe whose projecting sharp metal struts were curved in the shape of the continents—the Powell corporate logo. The ball was studded with bright lights, an electric beacon.

The missile motif was continued north of the arena, at the Boardwalk side of the Millennium. The casino-hotel was set back from the wooden walkway, and the grounds between them were still under construction. The site was fenced in, with big signs in front proclaiming, "Gilbert Powell's Millennium," and "The Millennium is Coming."

When the work was done, a long people-mover tube in the shape of a rocket ship would connect the casino-hotel directly to the Boardwalk. The mouth of the tube that opened onto the Boardwalk was shaped like a rocket's tail, and the far end was shaped like its nose. Eventually an automated slideway would carry people from the seaside to the casino without them having to lift a foot, but for now the tube was empty and off-limits, sealed off at its Boardwalk end.

Theme-park resorts, like Caesar's all-Roman decor, or the submarine-shaped buildings and pirate ships and man-made volcanoes in Vegas were the hot trend in the gaming industry now, and Powell was working his Missile Man persona for all it was worth.

Powell was into brand-name identification. Always push the company name and let the people know who you are. That's why the TV crew was shooting an intro in front of the missile marquee bearing the well-known Powell globe logo.

It made a nice visual backdrop for Anthea, while she was doing her thing. She was an attractive thirty-year-old black woman, wearing a yellow slicker and rain hat and clutching a cordless microphone. The bright TV lights pinned her like prison-camp searchlights, forming a fan of brightness that looked solid in the driving rain.

They gave her the go and she launched into her spiel, shouting loud into the mike, "Good evening, everyone, and welcome to a Powell Pay-Per-View Television exclusive event! It's hard to believe, but tonight's heavyweight fight is the swan song for the grand old Atlantic City Arena, the final event ever to be held in this storied hall before it is gutted and completely renovated as part of Gilbert Powell's Millennium Hotel and Casino." She said Powell's name with the same reverence that an evangelist would bring to the name of Jesus Christ.

She went on, "I'm eager to go ringside along with fourteen thousand fight fans who have braved Hurricane Jezebel to—"

"*Cut! Cut!*" said a voice in the ear of the headset she was wearing. The rig gave her two-way communication with the PPV control booth inside the building.

The voice was that of the director, who was in the control booth, orchestrating the action via the remote video monitors. The crew had headsets, too, and took their cues accordingly.

Anthea froze, glaring at the camera, knowing the director was seeing her in real time on the monitor. She wanted him to know that she was pissed. Like he cared.

He said, "Anthea, they want you to call it a tropical storm, not a hurricane."

"But it *is* a hurricane."

"Yeah, and it's also a holiday weekend, so will you please just call it a tropical storm, please?" His voice buzzed in her ear like a fly trapped in a bottle.

"I love this town," she said. "They even spin the weather."

"Aw right, we gotta go live with this one, so don't screw it up."

Anthea wouldn't let it drop. "Why couldn't I do the intro from inside? Why do I have to stand out in a fucking hurricane like a fucking weather bimbo and—"

"Because it makes good pictures, darling, and that's what it's all about."

"Picture this," she said, giving him the finger. "Why do I have to do it? Why not Lou?"

Lou was Lou Logan, their anchor.

"Because his toupee would blow away," the cameraman cracked.

"That's not a toup, that's his real hair," the lighting guy said. The cameraman peeked out from behind his eyepiece and looked to see if the other was serious.

"You can stop sucking up now, Lou's not listening," the cameraman said.

A new voice piped into the audio circuit, resonant but peevish.

"I am too listening, and it's my real hair!"

"Knock it off, Lou," the director said tiredly.

"Tell them to knock it off."

"Everybody knock it off. We've got a fucking show to do here, people, okay? Please." After a pause, he said, "Something keeps moving behind the marquee. What is it?"

The cameraman shifted views to focus on the background, which was dominated by a huge banner hanging above the entrance, promoting the fight. It said TYLER VS. RUIZ. ONCE MORE. NO FEELING. It was a play on the old line, "Once more, with feeling," only the idea was that the contenders would go at it like a couple of stone-cold professionals—icy, emotionless punching machines.

Actually, the word was that there was plenty of feeling between the two—all bad. They genuinely despised each other and were going into the bout with a lot of real heat.

The banner was as big as the mainsail on a tall ship and about as well-rigged, but the storm was playing hell with it, booming and tearing at it, trying to rip it loose.

"It's distracting. Shoot around it," the director said.

"Okay," the cameraman said.

"And what's that pinging noise I keep picking up on the audio?"

"It's the marquee shaking in the wind."

Anthea, standing at the base of the tower, looked up. The missile posts shook and swayed with vibration. The closer to the top, the more they swayed. The round beacon globe was really bobbing around up there.

She involuntarily took a few steps away from it, and said, "Damn! Is this thing safe?"

"Sure, it's safe. Powell knows what he's doing. I just wish to hell somebody else around here did," the director said.

In a different, no-bullshit tone, he said, "I'm starting the count now. We're on in five—"

He counted down, while Anthea firmed up her stance and turned on the personality wattage, smiling brilliantly at the camera. Her makeup was flawless. It was the kind they use in Hollywood when they're filming underwater scenes.

"—three, two, one. Go," the director said.

"Good evening, everyone, and welcome to a Powell Pay-Per-View Television event! The lucky ones are already inside at the fight, as the first taste of Tropical Storm Jezebel lashes the Boardwalk outside the grand old Atlantic City Arena. . . ." Anthea began.

While Anthea was giving the intro, Lou Logan was down at the broadcast table at ringside, fussing with his hair. Beside the table stood a mobile cart with a couple of video monitors. The program monitor showed Anthea, while the preview monitor showed Lou checking out his image on the screen.

He stood in front of a ringside camera, continually glancing sideways at the monitor, studying his head as he tilted it at angles, frowning at the video looking glass.

He was a popular sportscaster in the Philadelphia–South Jersey market, who'd been picked up to anchor the PPV broadcast and do running color commentary throughout the fight. He didn't know much about boxing but they had a couple of ring experts on hand who would actually do the round-by-round coverage and analysis. As the anchor, Lou had the most important task, to do the announcing and hype for Powell Resorts International and its upcoming PPV events.

He had one of those big heads of hair found only on

TV announcers and game-show hosts, a big, elaborate sculpted pompadour that swept over and back to cover his scalp like a plastic helmet, with every hair in place. Except every hair wasn't in place. The humidity, which was virtually at one hundred percent, had caused his hairstyle to wilt like a leaky balloon.

Anthea was moving into the finish of her intro. Lou looked around frantically, and asked, "How're we doing on time? What do I got, like thirty, forty seconds? Where's Janeane, my hair's a mess over here."

Janeane handled the makeup duties, but she wasn't around right now. "She's busy, Lou," the remote producer said, sticking his head up from behind the hardware-laden cart. He ducked back down and resumed what he was doing.

What with 14,000 screaming fight fans packed into the stands, bad rock music blaring out of the public address system, and potential storm-caused technical glitches in the electronic hardware, he had his hands full. He didn't need problems.

Neither did the director, up in the control booth overlooking the ring, sitting at a board filled with flickering monitors. "Your hair's fine, Lou," he said over the headset.

"Um . . ." Lou said, doubtful. He flicked his finger-tips against the temples, smoothing the hair down.

A guy pushed into view, stood next to Lou and put an arm around his shoulders, grinning broadly at the image of himself sharing the monitor screen with the sportscaster.

Up in the control booth, the director did a double take, goggling at the newcomer, whose image was replicated on all the screens carrying the preview feed.

"Who the hell's that?!" he said.

A technician sat on his right, also working the board. The director gave him a "what gives?" look, and the former shrugged.

The scene-crasher was Rick Santoro. Lou knew him. They were buddies. He said, "Hey, look at this, I'm on TV!"

"Ricky, for Christ's sake, I'm on in thirty seconds," Lou said.

"Twenty," the producer called out from behind the cart.

Rick turned his head from side to side, profiling for the camera, eyeballing himself in the monitor's video mirror.

"I always wanted to be on television," he said, pleased. "I look good. I think people would vote for this face, don't you?"

"Voted 'Most Likely to be Indicted by the Grand Jury,' maybe," Lou said.

"Ha, ha. That's the only way you get anywhere these days, you gotta get your big fat smile all over the tube," Rick said. He smiled into the lens, showing plenty of teeth.

"Hi, Rick Santoro here," he said, trying it out for size. "Hello. Hi there. Richard Santoro, how are you?"

In the booth, the director was shaking his head. "Do you believe this guy?"

"Typical Jersey joker," the technician said, "a real wiseass. Probably mobbed up to the eyeballs."

With the director's voice squawking in the earpiece of his headset, the producer popped out from behind the cart. "Lou, could you ask your friend to please step the fuck out?" he asked, pleasantly enough.

Lou turned to one side, away from the camera. Out of

13

the corner of his mouth, he asked, low-voiced, "You down on the fight yet?"

Rick's eyes widened and he slapped a palm against his forehead, saying, "Shit, I forgot! You seen Jimmy George?"

"Yeah, in the tunnel ten minutes ago," Lou said. "Lay fifty for me."

"On who?"

"On who. That's a good one. On the champ, that's who. Tyler."

"Wow, the whole fifty?" Rick asked sarcastically.

"Fuck you then, a hundred." Lou dug into his pockets and fished out a hundred dollar bill, passing it to Rick. Rick made it disappear.

"Okay, big spender," he said.

On the program monitor, Anthea had wrapped up her intro and was starting the switchover to Lou. Rick was still on camera and the director was about to blow a fuse and was letting everybody on the audio circuit know it.

On the floor, the producer gestured frantically, waving for Rick to go away.

Anthea was getting set to make the handoff.

". . . to see IBF heavyweight champion Lincoln Tyler, an extremely popular figure in this area for his work with troubled youths, take on challenger Jose Pacifico Ruiz in a classic twelve-round confrontation between a counterpuncher and a brawler."

The producer gave Lou the count. "And five . . . four . . . three . . ."

"Isn't that right, Lou Logan?" Anthea said.

Rick ruffled Lou's hair, mussing it up beyond repair, then stepped off-camera an instant before the switchover.

Lou yelped, trying to straighten his hair just as the

camera light flared. The producer pointed, and Lou was on the air, live.

Lou was a pro and made an immediate recovery, effortlessly switching into full announcer mode.

"That's right, Anthea, and if you think my hair is out of control, wait'll you see the incredible ring action we've got coming up tonight," he said. "Welcome, everyone, to Powell Resorts International's Atlantic City Arena, for a night of world championship boxing!"

There was more, but Rick didn't bother to listen. He had already made his exit from the arena floor, entering one of the tunnels that led to the guts of the building. He had business to take care of.

Jimmy George was a bookie, a sloppy rumpled guy with a jowly hound-dog face. Rick spotted him coming out of one of the boxer's dressing rooms. The area was restricted to authorized personnel, and patrolled by blue-shirted private guards, members of Powell's security forces. They let Rick roam the halls free and easy as he pleased. Mr. Inside.

Of course, the same could be said of Jimmy George, too. In Atlantic City society, he and Rick were both *persona grata*.

Rick saw Jimmy George stepping out the door, into the hall. He hustled after him, calling "Jimmy George, wait up a second!"

When he heard his name called, Jimmy George froze, and stood there holding the handle of the partially-closed door. There was no joy in his face as he saw Rick hurrying up to him.

Glancing into the dressing room, Rick caught a quick glimpse of the champion, Lincoln Tyler himself. He was shadowboxing, showing off for a PPV video crew that was in the room with him, lensing a segment. Jabbing, hooking, up on his toes, moving like lightning, he was a blur of brown sable motion. Rick could hear the whoosh of punches whipping through the air.

In the room, a guy came to the doorway, a little wizened guy in a suit jacket and tie, balding, with a bony skull and big oversized glasses with thick lenses. They gave him a bug-eyed look, making his other features look shrunken. Scowling, he reached for the door.

"What're you looking at? You want to see the show, go buy a ticket," he said, slamming the door in Rick's face.

Rick was too excited to get teed off. "Linc Tyler, the Fury from Jersey, standing right in front of me. The champ! Were you talking to him?"

Jimmy George looked up at him from the tops of his eyes, the rest of his face immobile. "Do I ask you what you do at work?"

Rick was impressed. "No shit, the man bets on his own fights. Now that's confidence."

"What do you want, Rick?"

"What's up your ass?" Rick asked, frowning.

"I'm having a bad day. What do you want?"

"Five large on Tyler."

The bookie just looked at him. There was a long pause in which they were both silent, statue-still. Jimmy George blinked a few times.

"You got it on you? Let me see it," he said, too casually.

Rick was starting to get hacked off. "What're you, a bank now? I gotta put up front for the privilege of betting on a lousy fight?"

"Yes, you do. Take it or leave it, Rick, I don't need the aggravation."

Rick tried a different more wheedling, tone. "Aw, come on, have I ever stiffed you one time? Name one time?"

"No, you just take forever to pay, that's what you do. Five grand. I'll see that a year from next Christmas. Where you gonna get five grand?"

Rick, frustrated, said, "The guy's ten to one to win, I can't make any money if I lay less than that!"

The bookie shrugged. "I missed the part where this is my problem."

Rick's face hardened, as he got ready to get tough and make it Jimmy George's problem. He stiffened and the bookie flinched, sensing the raw potential violence in Rick about to flare to the surface.

The dressing-room door opened again, and out stepped a flashily dressed, shifty-looking dude. He paused in the doorway, turning to lean back into the room.

Rick and Jimmy George stood a few paces down the hall, where Rick had steered the bookie while he was trying to lay the bet. He looked over the top of Jimmy George's head at the shifty-looking dude, recognizing him.

The dude was standing in the doorway with his back turned to Rick, not seeing him. Rick grinned, the tension in the air between him and the bookie evaporating. He had bigger fish to fry. He looked smugly eager, like a bully who spots his favorite whipping boy entering the schoolyard.

"Christmas came early this year," he said, mostly to himself.

"Huh?" Jimmy George said.

The shifty dude was still in the doorway, saying something to somebody in the room.

"The best for the best, right, Mr. Tyler?" he said. That was his exit line.

Very discreet. Rick could have laughed. What a dickhead! The dude closed the door and turned, coming face to face with Rick bearing down on him.

"Hello, Cyrus," Rick said.

Cyrus was quick. Well, in his line of work, he had to be. Without a word, he turned and took off running. Rick took off after him.

Jimmy George watched them go, dwindling down the corridor and out of sight. He was still a little white around the eyes and nostrils, shaken by his brush with Rick's bad vibes. With all that backslapping buddy-boy stuff, it was easy to underestimate Rick, and that was a mistake, because when you got him riled up he could take your head off.

The bookie didn't envy Cyrus.

Cyrus ran fast, his footfalls pounding down the hall. Rick trotted after, loping along like a greyhound. Cyrus whipped around a corner, coming to an escalator. He clomped down the moving stairs, holding on to the side rails with both hands. At the bottom of the escalator, he took off running again.

A uniformed cop was posted nearby, standing with his back to the escalators. He didn't see Cyrus, but he heard him running away. He turned in time to see him disappearing down the left-hand corridor.

Rick came down the escalator, taking the stairs two at a time, making noise. The cop had started after Cyrus, then checked and reversed himself when he saw Rick, moving to intercept him.

He said, "Hold it, pal! Where you running to?"

Rick was already reaching into an inside coat pocket. The cop saw the move and started, putting a hand on top of his holstered gun. Rick might be reaching for anything, a weapon.

Rick pulled out a leather billfold and held it in front of him. He held his other hand palm-up, showing it was empty. He said, "Whoa!"

He flipped open the billfold, flashing his badge and ID. "Northfield Major Crimes Unit," he said.

He was an Atlantic City cop himself, a detective. The badge was a detective's shield.

The cop who'd stopped him was a rookie, a relative newcomer to the force. He had to be, or he'd have known Rick by sight, the way that just about everybody in town did—everybody who counted, that is.

The young cop was abashed, with a sickly grin. "Oh, shit, sorry, sir. You need a hand?"

"Nah, I got him," Rick said, bolting.

TWO

Cyrus was goosed by fear-driven adrenalin. Rick had greed going for him, and that was almost as good. Unlike Cyrus, he knew the ins and outs of the arena's subsurface levels, the intricate workings of its corridors and junctions. He knew where he was going and Cyrus didn't and that gave him an edge.

Cyrus just knew that he wanted to get away from people, Rick in particular, but all people in general. Where there were people there would be cops, and he didn't want any more of them taking up the chase. He shunned them, dodging into empty corridors, lost.

He kept running until he reached a dead end. The corridor was blocked by a blue-painted wooden construction fence. The fence was more like a wall, a solid barrier barring the way from floor to ceiling. In the middle panel, a tall oblong gate was outlined by a thin slitted crack. Like the rest of the wall, the gate was solid, opaque, except for a square hole cut in it at head height. The hole was big enough to fit an arm through, except it was covered by a chicken-wire screen.

The gate had no doorknob or handle, only a padlocked hasp at shoulder height that kept it sealed. Cyrus tore at it, but it was too tough for him.

What to do? He danced around, fists balled, saying "Fuck me! Fuck *me!*"

"You fucked yourself," Rick said, coming up behind him. "Kinda took a wrong turn somewhere, eh, Cyrus?"

"FUCK!"

Cyrus stood with his back to the fence, cornered. The only way out was through Rick, and that wasn't an option. Cyrus was no coward, but he was no fool, either. Tangling with a cop, any cop, was like playing against a stacked deck. And with a cop like Rick, the deck was all jokers.

He knew Rick. Who didn't?

He sagged against the wall, leaning against it for support. The chase had winded him. Rick was breathing hard, too. They were both sweat-soaked. Thanks to the storm, the air was super-heavy with humidity. Down here in the maintenance levels, the arena's air-conditioning was minimal. The air was so thick it could be seen haloing the lights, like mist. A man could break a sweat just thinking about moving.

Rick reached into a pants pocket and pulled out a key ring. It had a bunch of master keys on it, along with some picks and shims, what the law called "burglar tools," the possession of which was technically illegal. Rick wasn't much bothered by technicalities.

He tried a couple of likely-looking keys on the padlock and succeeded in opening it on the third try. He took the lock off the hasp and pushed the gate inward, opening it.

He grabbed Cyrus by the arm, holding him just above the elbow. It was true that cops really "put the arm" on their captives, as Cyrus knew well from numerous past experiences. At least Rick hadn't put cuffs on him. Yet.

Rick steered Cyrus through the gateway. He was afraid to put the padlock back in place, in case somebody should come along and relock the gate. When he stepped through the gateway, he placed the padlock on top of one of the fence's thick, wooden support beams. He back-heeled the gate door shut, so that it was flush against the doorway.

They were in a short, narrow passage, enclosed by wooden frame sidewalls and a ceiling, lit by overhead construction lights that hung on hooks from the rafters. The floor was a rubber-treaded ramp. The passage was more like a chute than anything else. It was a half-dozen paces or so long, opening onto another, larger space.

Rick hustled Cyrus through the chute, into a long, futuristic tube that met it at right angles. This was the rocket-shaped people-mover tube which, when completed, would connect the Millennium casino-hotel with the Boardwalk.

The tube was ten feet tall and as many feet wide, with a curved glass ceiling. To the left, it tilted downward to the Boardwalk; to the right, it rose gently to the Millennium. It was sealed at both ends.

The tube would ultimately be equipped with an automated slideway, a people treadmill like the kind used in airports. The floor was wide enough for one slideway, which would carry people from the Boardwalk to the casino. If they wanted to leave the casino for the Boardwalk, they could damned well walk.

There was enough ambient light from the arena, the Millennium, and the Boardwalk shining through the glass ceiling to illuminate much of the tube's length. The glow was murky and uneven, muddy with brown shadows, but there was enough light to see by, at least here at the midpoint of the tube, where the short passage connected it to the arena. The ends of the tube were in darkness.

Rain pounded on the glass ceiling, blurring it with endless sheets of water. Winds shook it. Scattered along the tunnel were piles of construction materials, wheelbarrows, and the like, as if the work crews had just quitted them and would be back any minute now to resume work.

It might as well have been a tunnel on the moon, or under the sea, as far as Cyrus was concerned. He was fucked. He yammered, "What—what—what do you want!"

Rick shook him until he shut up, then said, "What do you think, Cyrus?"

"No!"

"Yes!"

"Fuck you, it isn't fair!"

"Call a cop," Rick said. Before Cyrus could say "fuck you" again, Rick swung him around by the arm, bouncing him off the far wall of the tube. He held him pinned against the wall with one hand, and started going through his pockets with the other, turning them inside out.

Cyrus's sense of unfairness got the better of him and he knocked Rick's hand away. More surprised than angered, Rick put a finger in the other's face, in warning. Cyrus knocked that away, too.

Give a guy a break, and see what happens—Rick's face hardened, setting in grim lines. Time to get to business. He slapped Cyrus across the face a couple of times, bitch-slapping him, just to show he could do it. Cyrus's head rocked with the blows, going one way when Rick openhanded him, then the other way when he was backhanded.

Cyrus put his hands up to guard his face and Rick kneed him in the balls. It was brutal, and meant to be. Cyrus' face turned lead-colored, his eyes dull marbles, his open mouth sucking for air. He folded up, groaning. His knees gave and he slid slowly down the wall and sat on the tunnel floor, holding himself.

Rick took a step back, glowering. "You got the wrong attitude about all this, Cyrus."

He reached down, manhandling Cyrus, tearing the jacket off him. "See, when we have these little visits, I *allow* you . . ."

He turned the jacket upside down and shook it. Glass vials tumbled out, cascading to the floor, clinking when they hit. Inside the vials were off-white and dirty yellow rock crystals.

"I *permit* you . . ."

Rick shook the jacket harder, and out flopped a nice fat wad of cash, falling to the floor with a weighty thud.

"I give you the *opportunity* to pay for the extra police work that you create," Rick said.

He picked up the wad, balancing it on his palm, eyeing it. It was a roll of Bens, Ben Franklin hundred dollar bills—about three grand total, he figured. Nice.

"Doesn't it feel nice to contribute something to society for a change?" he asked.

Cyrus had managed to struggle into a kneeling posi-

25

tion. He hugged himself, head bowed, looking up with pain-filled eyes. The pain deepened as Rick stomped the glass vials one by one, grinding them underfoot.

When the last vial had been pulverized, Cyrus said, "What . . . Wha'd you do that for, man?"

"Penalty tax, for making me chase you, and for making me kick your ass to remind you about the facts of life, Cyrus."

Cyrus rolled back into a sitting position with his back propped up against the curved wall of the tube. He was still holding his balls.

"You're a hypocrite, man. What makes you think you're any better than me?"

Rick answered the question as honestly as he could. "Friends, Cyrus. Who doesn't like Ricky Santoro?"

"Not counting you right now," he added quickly.

He turned and went out the passageway, leaving Cyrus where he was. He went through the gateway and closed the gate behind him, leaving it shut but unlocked. He retraced his route through the tunnels, leaving the construction site behind.

Too bad he had to be such a jerk, but it was Cyrus's own fault. He shouldn't have run, and once he was caught, he should've had the smarts to submit to the shakedown with good grace. That's how the game was played. What the hell, Rick was a cop, with a badge and a gun. He could've blown Cyrus away in cold blood and come out of it with a departmental citation for bravery for defending himself against a crazed drug dealer.

Not that he would've, of course. Rick was a nice guy, as long as nobody fucked with him or tried to hold out. Hell, Cyrus had gotten off easy. A roughing-up and a hit

26

to the pocketbook was better than getting popped on a drug-dealing bust.

He counted the money as he walked, humming to himself. Three grand total, just as he'd guessed.

"Wow! Am I good!"

THREE

Rick ran into Jimmy George coming down the escalator that he had chased Cyrus down earlier. When the bookie reached the bottom, Rick steered him to one side, saying, "Just the man I was looking for!"

"I waited around for you but you didn't show. I figured you weren't coming back," Jimmy George said.

"I'm back. Hell, I never left." Rick pressed the wad of bills into the bookie's hand. "Three grand on Tyler."

Jimmy George didn't look surprised, he didn't look not surprised. He stayed poker-faced, as usual. He looked around to make sure no one was watching. He did it mostly with his eyes, with minimal movements of his head. The cop who'd intercepted Rick during the chase had gone somewhere else.

Jimmy George glanced down at his palm and the money wad in it. He blinked a couple of times, then squinted. He peeled the top bill off the roll, holding it carefully by a corner, pinched between thumb and forefinger, and held it up.

It was smeared with blood—Cyrus's blood. It wasn't a gory mess, but it was unmistakably bloodstained.

"Oops," Rick said, unfazed.

"Twenty-nine hundred. I don't want this one," Jimmy George said.

"Why not?"

"It's got blood all over it!"

Rick shrugged. "So what? Money is money."

The bookie shook his head. "I don't want it. It's jinx money."

"Christ, aren't you delicate." Rick took the bill and stuffed it into his shirt pocket.

To his left, a tunnel led to the arena floor. Suddenly, the arena lights dimmed and dramatic music started up on the P.A. system. Cops and guards cleared the tunnel of people. It was time for the fighters to make their entrance.

There was a clamor on the escalator as a group came down it. A fighter's entourage. There were managers, trainers, cornermen, a cut man, bodyguards, hangers-on, and flunkies, and there was the champ, Lincoln Tyler, the star around whom they all orbited. It was quite a crowd that came streaming down the escalator.

The group started for the tunnel. Rick stood against a wall, watching them. He went to say something to Jimmy George but the bookie wasn't there. Rick was mildly surprised, he hadn't seen him go. But the bookie was a slippery guy.

No matter, Rick had already laid down his bet. He remembered that Lou Logan had wanted to get down a hundred dollars' worth, but it was too late now. Tough.

That crack about "jinx money" irked him. He wondered if Jimmy George really believed that crap, or if he just didn't want to get his hands dirty with the bloody bill. He probably believed it, otherwise he would have taken the money. He was a greedy bastard. He was probably superstitious—like most gamblers.

All thought of the matter vanished in the excitement of seeing the champ. Linc Tyler came striding by, so close that Rick could have reached out and touched him. Tyler was well-proportioned, and it wasn't until you saw him surrounded by other people that you realized how huge he was. He wore a long-sleeved warm-up robe with a hood, the hood pulled up over his head, covering it like a monk's cowl. A warrior-monk.

Rick said, "Hey, Tyler, all right! Neptune High, check it out, right here!"

Tyler heard Rick, who was right on top of him, with only a couple of members of his entourage standing between him and Rick. Tyler glanced at Rick, blank-faced.

Rick held up his hand, showing his class ring. "Neptune High School! You and me, go Sea Devils, right?"

Tyler ignored him and moved on, toward the arena, taking his cadre with him. There was a gap between Tyler and his fight crew, and the group of his hangers-on. Rick stepped into the gap and joined the parade. Nobody challenged his right to be there. Maybe they'd seen him talking with Tyler and figured he was a pal. Whatever, Rick swept along through the tunnel, trailing in the champ's wake.

Then they were through the tunnel, emerging from its square-shaped mouth into the arena.

The arena was a vast, grand, vaulting space, big

31

enough to hold a battleship. A yellow oval floor was surrounded by concentric rings of seats, rising in terraced tiers to the roofline. The place was packed with a capacity crowd. The noise they made rose and fell like the sea. The air was close, stifling, steamy. A battery of boxcar-sized air-conditioning units was working overtime, but between the storm and 14,000-plus bodies jammed into one space, the arena was as cool and dry as a dinosaur swamp. Not that the fans gave a damn.

The house lights were low. A spotlight shone down from above, pointing a finger at Tyler as he came into view. His entrance music on the P.A. sounded like a cross between the *1812 Overture* and the "Theme from 2001," only funkified. It was drowned out by the crowd din, a roaring blast of noise.

Tyler and his followers went down a ramp to the arena floor. The floor was the eye of the storm, and in its center stood the cool, clean geometry of that squared circle, the boxing ring.

The big fights are orchestrated as elaborately as rock concerts, and this one was no exception. Strobe lights flashed, smoke clouds puffed up in pillars, laser light beams cut and thrust.

The champ and company went down an aisle, toward the ring. Rick was still with them, loving the fanfare, eating it up. Something buzzed against his side.

It was his cell phone, which had a vibrating buzzer to alert him to incoming calls. He spent a lot of time in noisy clubs and casinos and gin mills, places where he couldn't always hear a chirping beeper.

He pulled the cell phone from his jacket pocket. What a place to take a call! That's why he took it, so he could tell somebody, anybody, where he was right now.

It was his wife, Angela.

"Hey, hi babe," he said. "I can't talk right now, let me call you back in an hour or two."

"You don't want to talk to me, maybe you'll talk to your own son," she said.

"Let him go to sleep, I'll talk to him in the morning."

"Why not now, Ricky?"

"That's why," he said, holding the phone out to the noisy pandemonium of the arena. "Just tell him I love him and I'll—no, Angela, don't . . ."

A pause, then, "Hi, Dad?"

"Hi, Mikey," Rick said, his tone brightening. "I know. I know she is. . . . I know. It does suck. . . . Because it's a free country. No. No. You know why, so don't ask me again or I'll cut your head off and put it in the freezer for a week, okay? . . . I love you too. . . . No, don't—"

Don't put your mother back on, was what he was going to say, only Angela came back on before he could get the words out.

All this time, he'd been approaching the ring, and the noise was getting louder and louder. It was hard to make out what Angela was saying, but he got the idea that she wanted to know when he was coming home.

"Late," he said. "I don't know, late. Later than that . . . Yeah, sure, if they're open. With cheese? I don't care. *I don't care.* Cheese it is. Fine."

That settled, he hung up the phone and pocketed it. The crowd was in a frenzy as Tyler neared the ring. A bunch of state cops were standing at ringside, and they moved to clear the way for the champ and his entourage.

A guy in an aisle seat jumped up as Tyler came past, a beefy red-faced guy holding a horse-bucket-sized cup of beer. He leaned out in the aisle, getting as close to

33

Tyler as he could. He cupped a hand to his mouth and started yelling.

"You're goin' down, Tyler, you suck, man, you're goin' *down*!"

His bawling mouth was big enough to stick a fist into, and Rick would have liked to have done just that. *Asshole drunk,* Rick thought. The slob had yellowed teeth like rotten niblets of corn. He kept running his mouth, heckling Tyler, who couldn't seem to take his eyes off him.

Tyler reached the end of the aisle, passing the front-row seats as he entered the open area around the ring. He climbed into the ring.

The ring was crowded with various officials and personnel, including a tuxedo-clad announcer whose voice was miked into the P.A. system.

He said, "Ladies and Gentlemen, welcome to the Atlantic City Arena, soon to be part of Gilbert Powell's Millennium Hotel and Casino on the Boardwalk in Atlantic City, New Jersey!"

His delivery was hammy, like a circus ringmaster's.

"Tonight, Powell Pay-Per-View Television and Gilbert Powell Productions present world championship boxing, twelve rounds for the International Boxing Federation heavyweight belt!

"This bout is presented with the approval of the New Jersey State Athletic Control Board and boxing commissioner Nick DiBalistreri. It is sanctioned by the International Boxing Federation, at ringside, president Michael Lee. The ringside supervisor is Bill Brennan. The three judges for this contest—John Stewart, Peter Shane, and Rocky Cascalante. Chief ringside physician, Dr. Stanley

Addis; the timekeeper, Roosevelt Gilbert; and the referee is Frank Rotundo."

The introductions went on forever, like the credits at the end of a big special-effects-laden movie. Rick peeled off from Tyler's clique and made his way toward a ringside seat.

Sitting in the second row was a pair of heavyweights of a different kind, Gilbert Powell and Charles Kirkland. Powell, fifty, was iron-haired, craggy-faced, impeccably tailored, larger than life. Kirkland was in his sixties, white-haired, distinguished. He looked like the senior partner of a successful banking firm, which he had been until his recent government appointment. Now, he was secretary of the Department of Defense of the United States of America.

Hovering around Powell and Kirkland like bees guarding honey was a team of plainclothes security agents. A pair of them moved to intercept Rick as he neared their area.

They were big guys, fit, young but not too young, clean-cut. They were built like professional athletes and carried themselves well, with quiet stone-faced competence.

They stood shoulder-to-shoulder, blocking Rick's way. Before he could go into his spiel, a voice from behind them said, "It's okay, he's with me."

The two stepped aside, revealing the speaker standing behind them, Major Kevin Dunne. He was tall, trim, confident, a winner. He had a frank, open face and clear, keen almond-shaped eyes. He was flawlessly groomed and dressed. He wore a military-style uniform, but not one of any service branch that Rick recognized. The outfit was natty, custom-tailored.

"That's the man I want," Rick said. "Boys, do your duty, arrest him!"

The two agents paid no attention to Rick. Dunne gave a small, almost imperceptible nod, and they moved away, though not too far away, and went back to protecting their VIP charges.

Dunne looked at Rick, shook his head. "Would it have killed you to dress like you've got some class?"

"In case you haven't noticed, there's a fucking hurricane outside," Rick said.

He and Dunne went into a clinch, hugging and slapping each other on the back. They were old buddies, going way back. Way, way back. They had known each other from boyhood days, growing up on the streets together. Best friends all the way through high school and beyond. Kevin had joined the military and Rick had joined the cops, and they went their separate ways, but they were still tight, even after all these years. Rick loved him like a brother. No, better—he'd seen some of the things brothers could do to each other.

Dunne asked, "Where the hell have you been? I thought you were going to miss it."

"Police business," Rick said, thinking of Cyrus and Jimmy George, and smiled. "You know me, always working. When'd you get in?"

"Last night. Flew direct from New Mexico with Powell and the secretary."

"What were they doing there?"

"Sorry, that's classified."

"Fuck you. That's not classified," Rick said. He and Dunne grinned at each other. Rick glanced at the power duo in the second row.

36

"That Kirkland?" Rick asked, nodding toward Powell's companion.

"Tuck in your shirt and I'll introduce you," Dunne said.

"I wouldn't want to embarrass you and blow your gig, Kevin. Don't you want to check my security clearance or something? You on duty?"

"You're damned right I'm on duty."

Rick looked at him. "What, you got something?"

Dunne nodded. "Yeah, we've had a few threats lately. I decided to run this one myself. First couple months with a new guy, the nuts always come out of the woodwork. And with a published schedule, you can't take any chances. . . ."

"Come on, I want to make one more circuit."

Dunne started around the ring, making his inspection tour, Rick following. In the ring, the announcer was still droning on, making more introductions.

"Ladies and Gentlemen, please join me in welcoming our special guest tonight. Himself a silver medalist in the biathlon at the 1960 Olympic Games and now the distinguished secretary of defense of the United States of America, Mr. Charles Kirkland!"

The crowd applauded politely, bored. Kirkland rose awkwardly from his chair, half-standing, acknowledging the crowd with a tight, uncomfortable wave.

Dunne stopped walking around the ring. He shook his head, exasperated. "Great idea. Put a flashing light on your head while you're at it."

"At least they didn't boo him," Rick said.

"Never boo a guy who can call a nuclear strike down on you," Dunne said.

Kirkland sat down fast. "And seated next to the

37

secretary, a man who needs no introduction," began the announcer, before going into his introduction.

"The founder of Powell Aircraft, head of Powell Resorts International, and chairman of all allied Powell industries — your host for the evening, Mr. *Gilbert Powell*!"

Powell rose, smiling and waving to big cheers. He seemed to swell visibly, as if he were soaking up all that high-volume approval like a sponge. He reminded Rick of a statue he had seen once in a museum, on a grade-school field trip. It was a bust of an old Roman general. Or was it an emperor? Either way, Powell reminded him of it.

Dunne worked his way around the ring, his eyes in constant motion, scanning the sight lines, exits, avenues of approach — every factor that might impact his mission.

He came up behind one of his men, an agent posted on the floor outside one of the ring corners. The guy was in civilian clothing, but even from behind Rick could tell he was an agent, from the pro athlete's physique he had in common with the pair that had braced Rick back at the VIP zone.

This guy was watching the announcer when Dunne came up to him. "Eyes front," Dunne said. "What do you think this is, Friday night at the fights with your buddies?"

The agent was sheepish. "Sorry, sir."

"Take the west exit, I'll stay in the box with Top Guy."

"Yes, sir." The agent turned, crossed to a flight of stairs, and started climbing them. Dunne took something out of his pocket and held it so that Rick could see it. It was something like a kid's handheld video game, with a square, flat screen and a cluster of buttons and knobs. On the screen, eight tiny blips were moving around on a grid-square.

"Check this out," Dunne said. "It's a locator. Every agent wears one of these roach clips"—he pulled back the lapel of his suit, showing a tiny alligator clip with a match-head-sized clear plastic bead on it, attached to the underside of the lapel—"and we can download the floor plans of any building we're in. See that blip? It's the guy I just sent to the doors."

Dunne pointed to the agent who had just left, entering a tunnel at the top of the stairs. On the video screen, a blip cruised steadily down a clear space in the middle of a floor plan.

"You're a regular James Bond. I'm impressed," Rick said. "Man, you sure have come a ways from when we were kids working on the beach, lugging those big-ass umbrellas around in the sun, sweating our balls off."

"I was working. You were usually off under the Boardwalk with some babe," Dunne said.

"Yeah, that sounds about right."

"How's Angela?"

"She's fantastic. Fat. I love her," Rick said.

"How's the other one? What is it, Candy, or Tiffany or—"

"Monique. Skinny. Mean. Expensive. I love her."

Dunne laughed, shaking his head. "You gonna stay a few days?" Rick asked. "We got plenty of room."

"Are you kidding? I hate this town even when there's not a hurricane. When we flew in, I thought the ocean was going to reach up and suck me in, just for spite," Dunne said.

Now the announcer was introducing Ruiz, the challenger.

"Fighting out of the blue corner, wearing the white trunks with black trim and weighing in at two hundred twelve and one quarter pounds, from Mexico City, Mexico . . ."

Dunne had just about completed his circuit of the ring and he and Rick had neared where they started. Dunne said, "You have two kids, a house in Margate, a girlfriend in an apartment . . . on a cop's salary?"

"I saved my money and skipped a lot of lunches," Rick said. "What are you, my conscience?"

"You could use one." Dunne looked owlish. "Angela have any idea about Monique?"

"Get real. Everybody's happy, trust me."

"Angela's not happy, she's just uninformed. Maybe if she knew the rules she could play the game, too."

"Buddy, if Angela knew the rules, there would be no game. Rule number one is Angela can't know all the rules."

"It's gonna end bad, Ricky," Dunne said, sighing.

FOUR

"Choice seats, huh?" said Dunne.

"They're okay," Rick replied.

"Okay? You're sitting in the front row ringside!"

"Yeah, they're okay."

Not only were they in the front row, they were sitting directly in front of Powell and Kirkland. For security reasons.

"If you won a free car, you'd be bitching about having to pay the insurance," Dunne said. All the time, his eyes were restless, moving, appraising. He shifted in his seat, looking around. His gaze fell on a redhead sitting across the aisle from him, and lingered.

She was a beauty, in her early twenties, with a model-like face and a lithe, shapely body. Her hair was a shade of red not found in nature—fire-alarm red. Flashy, like her tight, skimpy dress and high-heeled shoes.

Dunne looked away, then looked back again. Rick

turned his head to say something to the other, then saw where Dunne was looking, and at whom. Rick looked at her, too.

"That seem right to you?" Dunne asked, tight-mouthed.

"That seems perfect to me," Rick said feelingly.

Dunne wasn't satisfied. "Who's she with? Not that guy next to her. A beautiful girl, all alone at a fight?"

"Getting better all the time."

In the ring, the announcer was moving into his big finish. "Fighting out of the red corner, wearing the solid black trunks, weighing in at two hundred eighteen and one quarter pounds, with a professional record of twenty-six victories, seventeen by knockout, with only two losses, recognized by *Ring Magazine*, *Fight Game Magazine*, and the International Boxing Federation as the heavyweight champion of the world—the Fury from Jersey—Atlantic City's favorite son, LIN-COLN TYYYYYYYY-LER!"

Rick and Dunne settled into their seats and got set for the opening bell.

"You gotta get out of this town, Rick. You know that, don't you?"

"Here we go again."

"I mean it, you come down to Washington for two days and I can line you up half a dozen interviews like that!" Dunne snapped his fingers. He said, "Everybody I went to the Point with has major juice by now, all I need to do is pick up a phone."

"You can't help yourself, can you?" Rick asked.

The fight instructions were over and the handlers had cleared the ring. The boxers stood bouncing in their corners, waiting for the bell.

Dunne wouldn't let it go. "Defense Protective Service

pays about double what you make in the first year. And the money's clean, Ricky. It's clean."

"No, thanks. I hate uniforms."

"You don't have to wear a uniform!"

Rick got a kick out of seeing Kevin get so worked up. "Don't worry about me," he said.

"You're right, it's too late for you, but at least don't make the kids grow up here. This isn't a beach town any more; it's a sewer."

"It's a gold mine. Anyway, what's wrong with Atlantic City? I like this town."

"You would," Dunne said sourly.

"I've got my world in the Boardwalk, everybody knows me. I got the whole town wired. Some day, if I manage to get my face on TV a few times, maybe I'll run for mayor or something, but that's as far as I wanna go."

"You know, I think you actually mean it," Dunne said, wondering.

"I was made for this place."

"You're better than you think, kiddo."

The opening bell sounded and the fight was on. The fighters came out of their corners. Tyler had thick, strong limbs and a blocky torso, a classic heavyweight's build. Ruiz was pumped throughout his upper body, with a tapering V-shaped torso. He was good-looking in a sneering way, with a lot of female fans.

Tyler advanced, methodical, relentless. Ruiz was a dancer, bobbing, weaving, sidestepping the champ. Tyler kept stalking him. Suddenly Ruiz lunged, and there was a quick flurry of blows, ending before the crowd could get too excited by them.

Rick leaned forward, intent. He was a big fight fan and

besides, there was nothing like getting down on the match for three grand's worth to keep it interesting.

Dunne was less into it. He was not bored, but restless. He kept scanning the scene, looking at the big picture, measuring, calculating options.

He looked at the redhead. Something about her didn't fit the pattern. She was edgy, fidgeting. She glanced around nervously, and saw Dunne looking at her. She was used to being looked at by strangers, strange men. She gave him a quick flirty smile and looked away. Dunne frowned.

He leaned over to Rick, nudging him. "She's not even watching the fight."

Rick was. He nodded, not hearing Dunne. He didn't notice Dunne getting up and leaving, because he was too into the fight.

Dunne crossed the aisle and spoke to the redhead. She answered. There was a sound of leather fists thudding on flesh in the ring, and the crowd was roaring. Dunne looked away, and when he looked again, the redhead was gone.

He looked around and saw her walking away, and started after her, up the opposite aisle toward the tunnels.

Tyler churned the air with his arms but he couldn't seem to connect with Ruiz. Ruiz kept slipping him, dancing away. He was trash-talking, too, working his mouth harder than he was hitting as he kept circling around Tyler.

Rick turned to say something to Dunne and saw that he was gone. He looked around, his cop eyes working, just in time to see Dunne climbing to the top of a flight of stairs opposite their seats. At the top of the stairs was a tunnel mouth. All the tunnels were numbered, marked with big black numerals a couple of feet tall. This one was Tunnel 26.

Just outside the tunnel mouth, Dunne caught up with the redhead. There was no mistaking her, that bright red hair would have stood out a mile away. Not to mention that hot body in the skimpy dress.

Dunne and the redhead entered the tunnel together, disappearing into the shadows.

Rick sat back, grinning. He didn't blame Dunne for tailing the redhead. That was some tail. So, despite his all-business attitude, Dunne wasn't entirely a Boy Scout. It was good to know that some things don't change.

FIVE

A few seconds after Dunne and the redhead went into the tunnel, out came a woman in white, into the light. A blonde, slim, in a neat, white suit. She paused, looking around uncertainly, looking everywhere but at the ring. She glanced down at where Rick was sitting in the front row. Behind Dunne's empty seat, she could see Secretary Kirkland, sitting in the next row. She started forward, then checked herself, standing in the same place, waiting, watching.

A guy in a suit came down the aisle, halting at the second row, motioning to get Powell's attention. It was one of his aides. The guy caught Powell's eye, gesturing to him, getting across the idea that Powell had a phone call. Powell excused himself from Kirkland, got up, and followed the aide down the aisle and away.

Up near the tunnel, the blonde in the white suit saw

him go. When he was out of sight, she went down the steps, not hesitating now.

A latecomer was wandering the aisle, ticket stub in hand, peering this way and that. He started toward Powell's empty seat, edging into the row. Kirkland glanced at him. The latecomer double-checked his ticket stub and realized he was in the wrong row. He eased back into the aisle, realized he was in the wrong section, too, and went away.

As he left, he brushed by the blonde in the white suit, who was making a beeline for the front row. She sat down in Dunne's empty chair, directly in front of Kirkland.

She was in her mid-twenties, with a blonde bubble hairdo that covered her forehead and the sides of her face. Tinted glasses hid her eyes. From what Rick could see of her face, she was cute, but she looked anxious, worried.

He leaned toward her and said, not unkindly, "That seat's taken."

"I'll just be a minute," she said, flinching.

Rick shrugged and went back to watching the fight. What the hell, it was a shame to waste a front-row seat at the fight, and since Dunne wasn't using it, somebody else might as well enjoy it, especially if that somebody was a young, pretty blonde. No wonder she was uptight, she probably thought he was going to bounce her out of the seat. Dunne could do that when he got back from doing whatever he was doing with the redhead, or trying to do.

It was early yet, not even the middle of the first round. Rick was a little disgusted—he'd never seen Tyler fight so bad. The champ couldn't seem to get anything going. He was probably pacing himself, carrying Ruiz, not wanting to finish him off too soon, so the fans would get their money's worth.

The blonde took off her suit jacket and draped it over the back of her chair, displaying a pert figure under her blouse. At other times, Rick would have been more interested, but not now, with the fight going on.

The jacket slipped off the back of the chair, falling in front of Kirkland. The woman turned around as he picked up the jacket and handed it to her. She leaned toward him and they started speaking, their words blanketed by crowd noise.

A Ruiz jab tagged Tyler's nose and the champ's eyes flashed. He loosed a short hard right that landed on the button of Ruiz's chin. Ruiz wobbled, his eyes glassy, and he dropped to his knees on the canvas.

The crowd erupted with cheers, Rick yelling as loud as anyone. The noise was no different from the clamor made by the crowds in the Colosseum two thousand years ago that watched the gladiators chop each other up.

The roar lessened somewhat as Ruiz got to his feet, shaking his head. The fight continued, Ruiz still sneering, but not running his mouth anymore.

The blonde was chattering animatedly at Kirkland, explaining something to the secretary with great urgency. Kirkland's mouth made a small round O of surprise. He leaned closer, putting his head next to hers.

Across the ring, some loudmouth was standing up in front of his seat, shouting, with both hands cupped around his mouth like a megaphone. He had some pair of leather lungs, to be heard over the racket that the rest of the crowd was making. People seated nearby were turning in their seats to glare at him.

It was the same asshole drunk as before, the beefy

red-faced drunk who'd been ragging Tyler earlier, when he'd come to the ring. His voice had a raw, nasty sound that got on Rick's nerves, making him want to put the guy's head through a wall.

It must have gotten to Tyler, too. The champ closed with Ruiz, then got distracted, breaking his timing for a second. Ruiz lunged with a wild right hook that didn't even come close, slipped, and accidentally head-butted Tyler. At least it looked like an accident.

The head-butt opened up a cut over Tyler's eye, drawing first blood. The crowd responded like a cageful of lions at feeding time, right before the raw meat is tossed to them.

Tyler staggered, shaky, in trouble.

The drunk was jumping up and down, screaming, *"Here comes the pain, baby, here comes the pain!"*

Ruiz closed, letting loose with a murderous uppercut right straight at the point of Tyler's chin. Tyler's head snapped back, recoiling. He backpedaled into a corner, dazed, leaning against the ropes.

The crowd jumped to its feet, Rick among them. He could see his three grand bet going down the toilet. He shouted, "Up up up, keep your guard up, you idiot!"

Kirkland and the blonde alone seemed oblivious to the uproar. They were deep in conversation, their heads together. He was serious and solemn-faced, she was arguing vehemently.

Finally, she got so loud that Rick couldn't help hearing the tail end of what she was saying.

". . . *You're* the one who's going to be sorry!" she shouted.

That sounded like a threat. Rick took a second look at her. Just then, Ruiz charged Tyler, swinging wildly, pummeling him. Tyler's arms were up in front of his midsection, but his guard was down.

Ruiz banged a few into Tyler's head. The champ bounced off the turnpost and fell forward face-first, like a body falling out of a closet. He hit the canvas with a thud.

The crowd shrieked, screaming with bloodlust. Kirkland leaped to his feet to see the finish, and the blonde stood up with him, still talking.

A shot was fired, its dull, flat boom going off in the middle of the uproar. It sounded like a cherry bomb or M-80 exploding, but Rick knew it for what it was—gunfire.

Almost simultaneously with the shot came a meaty thwacking sound. It was considerably closer. In fact, it came from behind Rick.

It was the sound of a bullet drilling Kirkland through the neck. It must have struck an artery, because it sent a blood spray jetting into the air, splattering the front of the blonde woman's blouse.

She looked down at the blood, then at Kirkland, who was still on his feet, swaying, spraying blood from the hole in his neck. Then he collapsed, and she started screaming.

It wasn't the first time Rick had been around a shooting, and he knew that when one shot is fired, there's usually more to come. Instinctively he shoved the blonde to one side, out of the way.

A second shot tore over her shoulder, grazing her, tearing her blouse and the flesh beneath. There was a mist of blood, her blood. The slug kept on going, splintering the back of a chair and sending the shards flying.

51

Rick reached into his jacket and drew his gun, a flat black .9 millimeter automatic. He tried to look everywhere at once. Kirkland was down, sprawled on the floor between the rows, a pool of blood expanding outward from the hole in his neck. Rick couldn't tell if he was dead or alive.

The blonde was on her hands and knees, scrabbling around on the floor, reaching under the seats. She pulled a manila envelope from Kirkland's hand, then stumbled to her feet, clutching it to her.

She staggered toward the aisle, tripped, and fell. Rick grabbed for her, catching a fistful of blonde hair. Her hair came off in his hand. He froze, thinking it was some kind of grotesque freak wound, and that her scalp had been shot off her skull.

Then he saw that she had a full head of brown hair, and he knew that the blonde hair was only a wig.

One of Dunne's plainclothes Defense Protective Security agents was in motion, throwing himself across Kirkland's fallen body, putting himself between the secretary and any other bullets that might be fired.

The furor that had erupted when the champ was knocked down was nothing compared to what happened when people finally realized there had been a shooting. The spectators in Kirkland's vicinity threw themselves away from him, ducking behind the seats, dodging for cover. They barreled into those around them, knocking them down, creating a kind of domino effect. Panic spread like a gasoline fire, blazing up hot and fast.

Gun in hand, Rick jumped up on top of his seat for a better vantage point over the heads of the crowd. In his other hand, he held his billfold out in front of him with the badge prominently displayed. He didn't want to get shot by any security agents or cops who might mistake him for the gunman.

Working backward from where the shots had hit, he traced the bullet paths back to their likely point of origin. He didn't know if there was more than one shooter, or if both shots had come from the same gun.

Up in the mouth of Tunnel 26 was a little puff of smoke. Beneath it was a man in a ratty army jacket, pointing a rifle.

The assassin.

Rick had a clear shot at him. It was a hell of a shot to have to make with a pistol, but maybe he'd get lucky.

Before he could fire, there was a third shot. This one wasn't as dull and booming as the first two had been; it was more of a short, snapped *crack!* like somebody slapping a book down on a table.

It came from the tunnel, from behind the assassin. There was a bright yellow muzzle flare and a bang, and the assassin's head was outlined in a red halo and he fell forward and down, not moving.

Somebody had tagged him with a head shot from behind. From out of the mouth of the tunnel, Dunne stepped into view, a smoking gun in his hand.

Those who hadn't panicked from the first two shots stampeded at the third. People were screaming and flooding the aisles, trampling each other as they rushed for the exits.

In the ring, Tyler jumped to his feet, looking around wild-eyed. It was a hell of a comeback, considering the beating he had just taken. He saw Rick standing on a chair above the crowd, and for an instant they locked eyes.

The blonde—no, not a blonde—the woman in white

was up on her feet, getting away, holding the manila envelope clutched to her.

Rick yelled, "Hey, lady! Lady in white, are you hit?!"

She sure looked like she had been hit; there was a red stain spreading on her shoulder. She couldn't have been hurt too badly, or she wouldn't have been up on her feet and moving, not if she'd taken a solid hit from a high-velocity rifle bullet like the one that had downed Kirkland.

She glanced back at Rick but kept on going, pushing forward until she was swallowed up by the crowd. Rick hopped down and tried to follow her, but the mob surged and he couldn't make any headway through it. When he looked again, he couldn't see her—she was gone.

He said, "FUCK!"

He saw Dunne bulling his way forward through the crowd on the floor. He waved to attract his attention, shouting, "Kevin! He's down, The Man is down!"

Dunne went to Kirkland, and saw him sprawled on the floor in a pool of his own blood.

"Oh, Christ, no," Dunne said softly, his face white.

The security agent who'd been covering Kirkland now cradled the fallen secretary in his arms, trying to stop the blood flow with his hands. Kirkland was motionless, shrunken. Was he alive or dead? The wound was serious, perhaps mortal. The agent was shouting for a paramedic.

Rick doubled back, joining Dunne. He said, "That woman, in white, she was right next to him, she took a bullet and ran away, didn't you see her?!"

"No! What woman?" Dunne asked, shocked.

"It sounded like she was threatening him, she took something from him, too. Close the doors, man, she's headed out!"

Dunne grabbed the nearest of the blue-shirted arena security guards who were swarming onto the scene. He said, "Can you seal off the arena?"

"Huh? What do you—oh my God!" The blue-shirted guard got his first look at Kirkland. "Holy shit, he's dead, isn't he?!"

"GET ON THE FUCKING AIR RIGHT NOW AND SEAL OFF THIS ARENA, DO YOU UNDERSTAND?"

The guard got the message.

SIX

All over the building, inside and out, automatic machinery went into operation, closing doors, gates, and exits. The arena reacted like a ship taking on water, closing all the watertight doors. In this case, not water, but the crowd was being contained.

Inside it was pandemonium, chaos. The fans knew that there had been a shooting and they wanted to get away. A hurricane didn't look so bad now, compared to what was inside. In the back of everyone's mind was a vision of crazed terrorists firing into the crowd, massacring scores of innocents, as had happened before in other countries. The scared citizens rushed for the exits.

Julia Costello knew better, but so what? She was running for the exit, too. She was just as scared as anyone in the throngs, and with better reason. She was the woman in white, the one who'd been wearing a blonde wig for the rendezvous with Secretary Kirkland. Her real hair color was brown. Her hair was brown, her face was white, and her outfit was spattered with blood.

She let herself be carried along with the crowd in the lobby, toward the building's Boardwalk entrance. There were so many people there that nobody took any interest in her. They were all trying to get the hell out.

Standing on tiptoes, peering between a lake of bobbing heads, she could see the exit doors at the far end of the lobby. Before the forward edge of the crowd could reach them, they were slammed shut, one after another, by a wedge of blue-shirted guards who moved into position in front of them.

They halted the crowd, holding them back. They weren't playing, and they roughed up a few belligerent types hard enough to show everybody that they meant it. The rush was blunted and the crowd checked.

No exit that way. Julia stopped short, heartsick. She'd have to try to find another way out. She turned and started in the opposite direction. Now she was going against the current and people streamed past her toward the lobby, not knowing that it was sealed off.

She rounded a corner, clutching her wounded shoulder with one hand, trying to conceal the spreading red stain that darkened her blouse. Her front was spattered with Kirkland's blood, too.

She staggered, weaving. The initial shock of the wound was wearing off and pain was setting in, a dull ache centered in her shoulder that she could also feel throbbing through all the rest of her.

She felt light-headed, dizzy. That scared her. If she should faint from loss of blood—!

The fear gave her extra energy to keep moving. She

wobbled like a drunk, barely avoiding collisions with the fight fans who were going the other way.

A blue-shirted guard bumped into her, hard. The bone-jarring jolt almost made her pass out. She would have fallen if he hadn't grabbed her by the arms, steadying her. He said, "Hey, be careful," as if it was she who had bumped into him, and not the other way around.

"Let. Go. Of. Me," she said, pronouncing every word very clearly and carefully.

He saw the bloodstain on her blouse. "Hey, what—?!"

She saw the emblem badge sewn onto the left breast pocket of his shirt, with its globe logo and the legend, Powell Security.

She tore free of him. "I said let go of me!" He was stunned by her sudden outburst, and before he could react, she put both hands on his chest and shoved hard, knocking him off balance. He staggered backward into a knot of fight fans coming off a ramp and got tangled up in them.

Julia turned and ran, around a corner and up a ramp. Behind her she could hear the guard yelling *"Come back here!"*

But she got away, losing him in the twists and turns of the corridors.

SEVEN

On the arena floor, the scene was the same, only worse. The crowd, security forces, and the press combined to make it a complete madhouse. People swarmed the tunnels, some trying to get out of the arena, others trying to get in. Many of the fans were drunk, scared, or belligerent—or all three—and the ones who weren't were being carried along by the ones who were. The Atlantic City Police Department uniformed cops weren't hesitant about using their nightsticks. The blue-shirted arena guards didn't have nightsticks, but they moved hard and fast to crush defiance. There were more and better fights between the fans and the cops than had been seen in the ring tonight. Rick would have laughed if it wasn't so sick.

The epicenter of the disturbance was the downed secretary. The press that had been covering the fight, reporters and photographers, knew that the story of the year, maybe of their entire careers, had been dumped in their laps. They were trying to cover that story, while the cops and guards were holding them back.

A new factor entered the scene with the arrival of the paramedics, who came racing into the scene rolling a stretcher. There were four of them, preceded by Gilbert Powell himself, who guided the way. Ahead of Powell, a V-shaped wedge of security guards parted the crowd in front of them, opening up a channel in the mass of people.

Powell was waving his arms, shouting, "Get the hell out of the way!"

The guards' flying wedge cleared a route straight to Kirkland. Powell was right there in the middle of the fray, helping the paramedics load Kirkland's body onto the stretcher.

He straightened up, with Kirkland's blood smeared all over him. Wild-eyed, he grabbed the front end of the stretcher himself and started up the stairs, leading the way for the four paramedics, who were gripping the stretcher rails.

Powell was screaming orders. "Tell them to drive the ambulance right through the main entrance and into the arena tunnel! Clear those people out of the way, make a hole, we're coming through!"

At the mouth of the tunnel, Rick and Dunne watched Powell and the paramedics rush past, racing the stricken Kirkland out of the arena. They were trailed by a pack of the press nipping at their heels. All were swallowed up by the tunnel, with Powell still shouting orders.

Dunne was reeling. "He's gonna die, Rick, ten to one the man is going to die. . . ."

"Pull it together, Kevin."

"I was out of position, I opened up a sight line—*I was out of the box,* man."

"What box?"

"Four-foot invisible box around the Man. Two men have to be in it at all times, I—I stepped off, man." Dunne was white-eyed, haunted-looking.

Rick grabbed him by the arm and pulled him into the tunnel, away from everybody else.

"I know this is a real fucking tragedy and everything, but if you don't get your shit together in the next thirty seconds you are going to have one hell of a problem," Rick said, low-voiced, urgent.

"You are a *hero,* Kevin, do you understand what I'm saying? It's all in how you spin this."

Dunne was having trouble getting out of the starting gate. "What? What?" he asked, frowning fiercely.

Rick said, "You saw a suspicious character and you went to check it out, right?"

"Yeah."

"But by the time you got there he had done the dirty deed, so you took him out. End of story, *capisce?*"

"But I didn't see the guy," Dunne said, "I was following this girl, she had red hair, and—"

"Forget about the girl, this'll stand up. That's your slug in the shooter's head, isn't it?"

"Yeah, it's mine, but I wasn't—"

Rick held up a hand. "Don't tell me, just get it straight in your own head, that's all that counts."

Dunne got mad. "What the fuck are you doing? I'm not some beat cop needs you to plant a piece for him, who do you think you're talking to?!"

"Cops have these moments, they happen, and this one

63

is happening to you." Rick was patient, explaining the facts of life.

"What you say and do right this minute is gonna change the rest of your life. I'm sorry your guy went down, but don't go down with him. Go to confession later if you have to, but don't fuck yourself up now," he said.

Across the arena, another half-dozen or more cops came charging down toward ringside with a thunderous clatter.

"Those are state cops from the Division of Gaming Enforcement," Rick said. "They're gonna try to muscle us, but we can't let that happen."

"Why not?" Dunne asked, without heat, curious.

"Because if we're first contact when the feds get here, everybody writes from our report. Your story'll hold because we say it does."

"How long does it take the FBI to get to a crime scene around here?"

"They gotta come from Trenton. An hour at least, hour and a half with the storm. We just have to fight these guys off till then and you're in the clear. Okay?"

When Dunne didn't answer, Rick said "Okay?" again, harder. Down on the floor, the stage cops were closing in.

Dunne rubbed his face, sweating. "Jesus, I don't know."

"I do," Rick said. "If there's one thing I know, it's how to cover my ass."

The state cops had just finished surrounding the corpse of the assassin. From the way they were acting, you would have thought he was still alive and dangerous. The killer lay facedown with a melon-sized hole in the back of his cranium where Dunne's bullet had struck. His rifle lay on the floor, a few feet away from his outstretched hand.

Rick and Dunne moved into the scene. The high-ranking cop in charge of the state cops was heavyset, fiftyish, and wore plain clothes.

"Gordon Pritzker, Division of Gaming Enforcement," he boomed, self-important. "What the devil—"

"I know who you are," Rick cut him off. "Listen up. We got two men down, this one's dead. He's the shooter. The other is Secretary Kirkland, as in secretary of defense of the good old U.S.A."

"My God!"

"Kirkland caught one in the neck; the paramedics just wheeled him out."

Pritzker paused, calculating. His eyes narrowed. "Who are you guys?"

Rick badged him. "Northfield Major Crimes."

"Major Kevin Dunne, Defense Protective Service. I'm in charge of the secretary's security detail. I was—"

Rick jumped in. "He saw the shooter come into the arena and he went to check him out, but by the time he got there, the guy'd already fired. The major took him out."

Dunne and Rick exchanged looks, but Pritzker didn't catch it. After a pause, Dunne nodded, blank-faced.

Pritzker bought their story. "All right, I'll take it now," he said.

"Bullshit," Rick said. "This isn't my blood, it's the secretary's, I was sitting right in front of him. I'm a homicide detective and a material witness, this is mine about six different ways."

Pritzker's jowls colored, reddening. "A.C. cops got no

business in the casino, this is strictly DGE and state police. You know that, so what are you trying to pull——"

"We're not on the fucking casino floor, Gordo, and this arena ain't the Millennium yet, it's Atlantic City, New Jersey, and that belongs to Northfield," Rick said, smiling thinly.

Rick continued, "You want to help, Gordo? Go tell your men to get all the press people out of here, find a room out in the hall, and lock 'em in, we'll give 'em statements when we're good and ready. Get all those cameras out of here now, unless you want the secretary of defense's wife and kids to get a close-up look at his internal organs on the ten o'clock news," he said.

Pritzker's sidemen were indignant, but they looked to their chief to call the play. Pritzker hesitated, which meant that he lost, and that Rick had taken over the play.

Rick spotted three uniformed cops and waved them over. "You guys are metro? Make this whole arena a crime scene, nobody goes in or out till the detectives get here."

Pritzker thought he saw a handle there and tried to use it. "Are you the guys that told 'em to seal the doors? You can't hold fourteen thousand people inside——"

"Yes we did and yes we can, those are eyewitnesses, all fourteen thousand of them, we can detain 'em for as long as it takes to get every address and phone number *and* take their pictures, now that I think about it," Rick said, starting to get warmed up. Dunne took him aside.

Dunne said, "The woman, the one that threatened him, she might have fingered the secretary for the shooter. You said she took something from him, did you see what it was?"

"An envelope, a manila envelope."

66

"We gotta find her before she gets out. What did she look like?"

"Caucasian, late twenties, dressed in white. Wounded in the shoulder, bloodstains. She was wearing a blonde wig, had brown hair underneath. The wig's probably still lying around somewhere."

"All right, you stay here with every uniform you can get. I'll run a top to bottom," Dunne said.

He rounded up a cadre of about a dozen Powell security guards, blue shirts. "You guys, come with me!"

He took them down the tunnel and away. Rick noticed Lou Logan lurking around, trying to edge in.

"Lou, where's the control booth for your pay-per-view cameras?" he asked.

Lou pointed to a shoebox-shaped structure with windows, jutting out from the wall a hundred feet or so above the arena floor.

"Up there," he said. "Listen, Rick, I want to talk to you—"

"I gotta take a look at something," Rick interrupted, walking away. Lou tagged along, not waiting for an invite.

Rick headed off toward the booth, Lou falling into step beside him. "Hey, Ricky—"

"I said no press in the arena, Lou."

"I can see why you want the rest of those assholes outta here, but I didn't think you meant me, too."

Rick gave him a look, not breaking stride. Lou went on, "Don't shut down all the cameras, you know what kind of break this is?"

"What kind of a break did Kirkland get? You can't show this, all the blood on the floor. The guy's got a family, have a heart for Christ's sake."

"I won't shoot the tomato gravy, then," Lou wheedled. "C'mon, if somebody's gonna make statements, you gotta have one pool reporter to ask questions, that's how they always do it.

"Let me be the guy, Ricky. I can't tell you what it would mean to me, you think I wanna do this pay-per-view shit the rest of my life? You know how Dan Rather got his big break? The JFK assassination!"

Rick tsk-tsked. "You make me sick, Lou."

"And if you're gonna be on TV, don't you want your old pal asking you the questions?"

Rick gave a slight nod, as if allowing that there might be something to what Lou was saying, but he still wasn't convinced.

"Plus I can have two grand, cash, in an hour and a half," Lou said, low-voiced, tossing in what he thought was the clincher.

Rick said, "You media boys really are a pack of vultures. You're a disgusting human being."

Rick didn't say anything after that, just kept walking with Lou trotting along beside. Lou couldn't stand the silence and broke first.

"Five grand. In an hour."

"Congratulations, Lou, you're the guy. Hook up out in the hallway, I don't want to see one fucking TV light inside. This whole arena is a crime scene."

"You are the king."

Rick dug into his shirt pocket and dug out a hundred dollar bill and handed it to Lou. "Hey, here's your hundred back. I couldn't find Jimmy George in time to lay it down."

"Lucky break for you, considering. All bets are off, huh?"

Lou looked down at the bill and made a face. It was the bloody Ben, the hundred-dollar bill that was stained with Cyrus's blood. Lou stopped walking, coming to a dead halt.

Rick kept on walking. Well, at least he had gotten rid of that jinx money.

EIGHT

The pay-per-view booth was crammed with monitors, control panels, and half a dozen technicians. A sign above the monitors bore the Powell global logo and the words POWELL PAY-PER-VIEW TELEVISION. Large windows looked out and down on the arena, the ring only a stone's throw away. The monitors showed different views of the arena, including an overhead view looking down from the top of the ceiling.

The screens flickered and shifted like a massive eye twitch, making Rick's head hurt if he looked at them too long. If he focused on one of them he was okay, but all of them at once had a dizzying effect. No wonder the TV people were such dizzy bastards.

Rick badged them at the start, before anybody could get snotty. He corraled the PPV director and told him what he wanted. The others went about their business. They had plenty to do without gawking.

The director sat in front of a large switching console. Rick stood beside him, leaning over the console, one hand resting on top of the unit.

"The secretary of defense gets his head blown off and you want to look at the fight?" the director asked, looking up at him.

"I'm a big fight fan," Rick deadpanned. "Give me the uppercut, the punch that knocked Tyler back in his corner."

The director kept looking at Rick, staring him in the face and frowning, as if trying to remember where he'd seen him before.

It came to him. "You're the guy who messed Lou's hair up," he said.

"That's right."

The director shook his head sadly. "It was all downhill from there."

"How about that uppercut? As close in as you can get."

"Whatever you say."

The director pointed to the monitor, where the videotape was rewinding, blurred images of the fight arrowing toward the critical punch. The director set it for right before the moment when Ruiz unleashed the uppercut.

"That what you want?" the director asked. When Rick said yeah, the director hit the switch and the image started replaying itself in real time.

There was the champ, bleeding from the cut over his eye where Ruiz had head-butted him—Ruiz rushed, closing—there was the uppercut, rising like a rocket— Tyler's head snapped back from the force of the blow, the rest of him following as he backed across the ring into the corner.

Rick leaned in closer to the screen, his face underlit by

the monitor's phosphor-dot glow. "Lemme see it in slow motion."

The director rewound the tape, then started it once again, this time in slow motion. The fighters' images crawled across the scene, like they were battling underwater.

It took forever to get to the uppercut. Ruiz's gloved hand rose, driving upward at the end of a big forearm, climbing up and up, arching in on a relentless trajectory toward Tyler's chin—and missing. The uppercut fanned the champ but never connected. Ruiz hadn't laid a glove on him, literally, but Tyler reacted like he'd been clouted with brass knuckles. His head snapped away and he reeled backward.

"I'll be damned," the director said.

"Air ball," said Rick.

The bottled-up crowd surged through the building, searching for exits that weren't there. In an arcade beyond the lobby, things were so chaotic that a souvenir and concession stand had been left abandoned and untended by the vendors.

It was a godsend to Julia. She edged up to the stand, her face white from fear and blood loss, and scooped up a handful of T-shirts, tossing one over her bloodstained shoulder, covering the stain. She kept moving, snatching a souvenir jacket off the rack, an expensive blue satin baseball jacket. It was a kind of hit-and-run, snatch-and-grab situation, only taking a handful of seconds, and then she was on her way again, slinking along the wall, hurrying away, ready to break into a run if anybody raised a hue and cry.

Nobody did. A couple of kids had seen what she'd

done, and they ran over to the stand and raided it, scooping up big double armfuls of merchandise.

Some adults chased them away and started looting the stand themselves.

Trembling, Julia pulled on the jacket, crying out from the pain of moving her wounded arm. A few people turned to look at her, but she kept walking. She turned a corner and wandered into a line of people streaming down a corridor.

At the end of it was the gateway to the neighboring casino. The line was stalled at front, where a squad of blue-shirted guards were passing people through one at a time, after first taking their names, addresses—and photographs.

Julia turned away, sickened. A couple of blue-shirts saw her hurrying away, but were too far away to do anything about it, and then she turned into a hall and was out of sight.

A ladies' room swam up on her left. She saw it, changed course, and ducked inside. To her relief, it was empty, deserted. The overhead fluorescents buzzed and the tiling seemed too bright.

She stumbled into a stall and locked it, wanting to laugh at how ridiculously little protection that sliding lock gave her, but fastening it anyway. She didn't dare laugh. If she did, she might not be able to stop.

She shucked off the satin baseball jacket and hung it on a hook on the door. Her hands shaking so hard she could barely undo the buttons, she opened her blouse. The fabric was pasted down to her bloodstained shoulder, and she had to peel it off, gasping as she did so.

Forcing herself to look at the damage, she saw a deep gash where the bullet had grazed her. It looked like the

74

claw mark of some bird of prey. The bullet hadn't pierced her; it was only a flesh wound. *Only*.

She felt light-headed, and nearly passed out from the pain. Her knees sagged and she started to drop. She saved herself from falling only by grabbing hold of a handicapped rail at the last second.

She pulled herself to a sitting position on the toilet. She felt very small and weak and helpless.

No, that's how they wanted her to feel. That wouldn't keep her alive. Her eyes narrowed and she clenched her jaw, and said stubbornly out loud, "You're not going to die. You're not going to die."

She tried to tear a strip of cloth off her blouse, but she didn't have the strength in her hands to get it started, so she took hold of a corner of fabric between her teeth and pulled until it tore. After that, she was able to rip a number of long cloth strips from the blouse.

She would have liked to have cleaned the wound at the sink but she didn't dare risk it. She folded one of the T-shirts a couple of times into a multi-layered pad, and placed it over the wound. She winced, and tears started from her eyes.

The pad would serve as a kind of absorbent bandage. The long cloth strips would anchor it. She wound the strips over the bandage and under her arm, tieing it in place. She took another strip and repeated the process.

"You're not going to die, you're not going to die," she muttered under her breath.

The manila envelope that she had taken from the secretary was still with her, stuffed into the front of her pants, lying flat against her stomach.

"You're *not* going to die, you're *not* going to die. . . ."

75

NINE

In the tunnel, two bodyguards stood outside Linc Tyler's dressing-room door. Ignoring them, Rick reached for the doorknob. One of the bodyguards reached for it at the same time, his hand covering Rick's. His hand seemed as big as a baseball glove. He was a big bad dude with a prison weight-room physique. His face was the size and shape of a cement block, without the warmth. He was utterly humorless.

"Mr. Tyler is not in the mood to speak to anyone at this time," he said.

"See where your hand is? That's a felony," Rick said.

The bodyguard took his hand away. Rick went into the dressing room, closing the door behind him. Inside, there was a training table in the center of the room and a small wooden table off to one side with two chairs at it. Tyler sat in one of the chairs at the table, facing the door.

Nearby were two more bodyguards and the little wizened guy who had slammed the door in Rick's face earlier.

Tyler sat hunched in the chair, grim and glum, a robe draped over his big shoulders, the cut still open over his eye. He was sweating.

He eyed Rick, sizing him up. Rick returned the favor. There was a fist-sized hole in the wall to one side of Tyler.

Rick crossed to him, pulled out the other chair, and sat down at the table opposite Tyler. The bodyguards gathered themselves, but before they could move, Tyler checked them with a look and they backed off.

"How you doing, Linc? Good to see you again," Rick said, smiling pleasantly.

Tyler squinted at him, a ferocious squint. "I know you?" His voice was low, calm, almost sleepy.

"Rick Santoro." He showed him the class ring. "Neptune High. A fellow Sea Devil. Class of '78."

Tyler looked blankly at him. "I don't remember you."

Rick laughed in disbelief. "C'mon, you must have seen me plenty! My hair was long then, but whose wasn't?"

"Mine," Tyler said. "I don't remember you."

"Lincoln, you're hurting my feelings. And after I dropped three grand on you."

The little guy had been standing on the sidelines up to now, fretting and fuming, biting his tongue to keep from speaking out—but he could stand no more.

"I think it would show more respect if you addressed him as *Mister Tyler*," he said.

Rick glanced at him. "Who're you?"

"Mickey Alter, Mr. Tyler's lawyer," the cocky bantam said, swelling himself up.

"His lawyer, huh? You're gonna have your work cut out for you," Rick said.

The other exploded. "What's that supposed to mean?!"

Ignoring him, Rick spoke to Tyler. "I don't have to tell you, right? I saw Jimmy George, you know, the bookie? He was coming out of here before the fight. How much did you lose? . . . Or did you win? Know what I mean?"

Mickey Alter stopped sputtering long enough to say, "It wasn't his night, that's all."

"It wasn't his night," Rick repeated. "I'll say."

Tyler said, "The guy fought very furiously." He spoke thickly, slowly, as if carefully chewing out his words.

Rick didn't laugh in his face, not quite. "You've never been knocked out your whole career. I mean *ever*, since your first Golden Gloves in, what, 1980? I've seen all your fights, I'd know."

"You're gonna tell me about my career?" Tyler pointed to the cut over his eye. "He head-butted me. You ever get cracked in the head by two hundred pounds with a skull on top of it?"

"Sure, my last anniversary."

"It messes up your brain, so you can't think. I can't remember anything after that."

"Cut the bullshit, Linc."

Mickey Alter burst in again. "Let me remind you who you're talking to, detective. Mr. Tyler is a significant public figure, a pillar of the community. Keep that in mind, or this interview is over."

Tyler said to Rick, "That guy. The secretary. He's dead, isn't he?"

"If you have a question, Lincoln, let me ask it for you," Mickey Alter said.

"I just want to know if the guy is dead."

"Smart money ain't on him," Rick said, "unless he can live with a fist-sized hole in his throat."

He put his elbows on the table and leaned forward. "You know who you reminded me of out there, Linc?"

"I don't give a damn."

"Sonny Liston in '65. Remember? It was the rematch with Ali, right after he joined the Muslims and changed his hand from Cassius Clay. Malcolm has just got whacked and Sonny was paranoid that somebody'd come up blasting at ringside, so as soon as the opening bell ring, he went down. He didn't even wait for a punch, he just hit the canvas and stayed down for the count. That was the famous Phantom Punch, remember?"

"No," Tyler replied.

"That's what you looked like out there tonight."

"Okay," Mickey Alter said briskly, "Detective, either you arrest him or I'm going to ask you to leave."

Rick looked at him with mild surprise. "Arrest? You're the one who brought that up. What would I arrest him for?"

He turned to Tyler. "What would I arrest you for, Linc? Getting up too quick?"

"What?"

"What?" Rick mocked, imitating him. "Come on, I *saw* you, and you saw me. You wanted it to look like a knockout, but your reflexes are too good. When you heard the gunshots, you were on your feet in half a second. Not your fault, totally understandable reaction, but it kinda ruined the performance, don't you think?"

"The guy knocked me out," Tyler said. He sounded bored, but he was sweating harder than ever.

"I looked at the fight tape, Lincoln. It was the Phantom

Punch Part Two. The acting's pretty crummy, but the boxing commission might find it interesting. . . . And a split second after you go down, an assassin fires. Some coincidence, huh?"

There was a long silence. Tyler might have been sitting there asleep, but his eyes were open. Mickey Alter's eyes were black beads behind the centers of his thick-lensed glasses. The bodyguards were staring off at different corners of the ceiling, like strangers riding up in an elevator, trying to make like they hadn't heard anything.

"Everybody get out," Tyler said at last.

They got out, leaving him alone in the room with Rick. There was something bleak, almost forlorn about the almost-empty dressing room. It smelled of sweat, smoke, liniment and rubbing alcohol, aftershave lotion, and a lingering chemical smell that Rick recognized as cooked crack rock. The chemical smell was coming from a back room, off the large main room.

"Ruiz is punk, know what I'm saying?" Tyler began. "He's nothing, no punch, no snap, weak, no technique—"

"You threw the fight," Rick interrupted.

"If I say yes, can I make some kinda deal with you?"

"You don't need a deal. I don't give a shit, you pay me back the three grand I lost and I forgive you. But why'd you do it? You can't need the money, you gotta be worth millions."

"They said I was never gonna fight again if I didn't help 'em," Tyler stated simply. "They didn't tell me somebody was gonna die," he added.

Rick quivered, on the scent. *"They?* Who was it?"

"You listen to me, this is important. I didn't know they

were gonna kill anybody." Tyler's pointing finger jabbed the air as he spoke, underlining his words.

"What did they have on you?"

Tyler was silent. Rick said, "Whether you knew what you were involved with or not, Lincoln, a guy is dead. You don't need that on your head. Get rid of it, tell me what happened."

"Got a cigarette?"

Rick shook one out of a pack and Tyler took it, lighting up. He blew out smoke and started talking. . . .

Earlier that night, before the fight, the dressing room had been crowded with Tyler's clique, his sidemen and hangers-on. His camp was in an up mood, certain that he would have no trouble taking Ruiz. The only worry was that Tyler would finish him off too soon, leaving the fans feeling that they'd been cheated. But so what? A win was a win, and money was payday.

Tyler knew better, but he wasn't talking. He wasn't in an up mood, though, but since he usually looked pissed off at the best of times, nobody noticed anything.

It was a regular party in the back room, where some sexy babes and smooth players were hanging out, getting high. The flash element was attracted to the champ and vice versa. Not that he'd ever get high before a fight—he was in training. Plus, there were drug tests. But if he'd ever wanted to get high before a fight, tonight was the night. Because Tyler was feeling low.

In the back room, Cyrus was holding court, that fool, cooking up some rock. He held a lighter that was like a mini blowtorch, jetting a spear of flame into the bottom of a thimble-sized metal mesh cup, holding the rock. The torch hissed, melting the rock and turning it into smoke.

One of the ladies crouched over it, sucking in the fumes and oohing and aahing like she was coming. A circle of others, smooth gangstas and whores, pressed in eagerly to take their turn.

Cyrus said, "Manna from heaven, baby, this is the real shit, nothing but the best, the best for the best. . . ."

Tyler was at the other end of the main room, as far away from the back room as possible. He didn't feel too sociable, but when the TV crew came into the dressing room to shoot him, he was glad to cooperate, because it gave him something to do. He shadowboxed for the camera, for himself, getting into it, loosening up.

Across the room, Mickey Alter was pacing back and forth in front of the party room, fretting, darting worried glances at it from time to time. And with a TV crew present!

But it was a Powell PPV crew, and they knew what not to get on video, so the little lawyer didn't have to sweat that one too much. But, still!

Alter closed the back-room door firmly, then went to Tyler and got him away from the TV crew, and said, "There's cameras everywhere, for Christ's sake! And what if the guy from the Athletic Commission walks in to check your gloves, huh? What're you gonna do, retire and live on your savings? What savings? You gotta have this freak show in here tonight, of all nights?!"

Tyler started shadowboxing again, throwing punches and jabs into the air, working up a sweat. Cyrus came out of the back room, rock fumes rolling off of him. He caught Mickey's eye and gave him the sign, rubbing his fingers together significantly. Fun was fun, but he wanted his money. His eyeballs were yellow, like a reptile's.

Mickey Alter rolled his eyes and went to get the money, cursing to himself. He crossed to a locker and unlocked it, taking his briefcase out. There was money in it, a lot of money, and he wasn't leaving it lying around unattended, not with some of the characters hanging around the champ's dressing room.

He turned his back to the rest of the room so nobody could see what he was doing. He reached into the briefcase and counted out three thousand dollars in hundred dollar bills. He folded the wad and pocketed it, closed the briefcase, and locked it up inside the locker.

He turned around, almost bumping into Jimmy George, who'd just stepped through the door.

"What do you want?" Mickey Alter asked.

The bookie cleared his throat, his baggy eyes guileless. "If I could just—for a second—I have a quick question, if I can just get a moment of your—"

"I'm standing right here, Jimmy. All you have to do is talk."

"I've been getting a lot of bets, very *large* bets, against Lincoln, that is, and I was just wondering, well, you know."

That kind of talk the lawyer didn't like. "Would you please lower your voice?"

"Everybody knows Lincoln likes the action, right? What I'm saying, he likes to gamble. Right? That ain't exactly a secret." He spoke in a low voice, though, so the lawyer couldn't kick about that.

"Never on boxing. Never on boxing! We went through all this shit with the commission, I don't have to explain it to you," Mickey Alter said.

"Uh, yeah, but he's in pretty heavy to some of the casinos, ain't he? And some people are sayin' maybe

Lincoln's lookin' to clean up the books, you know—like maybe he decided this ain't his night."

The lawyer got pious. "You actually came into a fighter's dressing room before a fight to tell him there's a lot of action *against* him? And then to have the gall to accuse him of . . ."

He continued, "I've never been so offended in my life. Come here, Jimmy, I want you to tell Lincoln what you just said to me. Come on, come over here. . . . Hey, Lincoln, Jimmy's got something to say to you!"

Jimmy George opened the door behind him, ready to exit. "Forget it, forget I said anything."

He darted out the door, right into Rick. But that was another story. Mickey Alter had gone to close the door, and wound up slamming it in Rick's face.

The lawyer went over to Tyler, still methodically slicing the air with punches. "You are never going to get away with this."

"'We,' Mickey. It's always 'we.' You told me that, remember?"

"We didn't get into this mess, Lincoln—you did. If you get caught, do me a favor and lose my fucking phone number. I told you you can't live like you do—you make yourself vulnerable. Everybody wants a piece of you."

He added, bitterly, "Well, they got all of you now."

Tyler went into a furious volley of air punches. One of them connected with the wall and crunched a hole in it.

Cyrus stood at the lawyer's side, grinning, waiting for the money. Mickey Alter passed him the three grand, which Cyrus stuffed into a jacket pocket.

Cyrus paused in the open doorway. "Nothing but the best!" he said. "The best for the best, right, Mr. Tyler?"

Tyler didn't answer. Cyrus, unfazed, waved so long and stepped into the hall, closing the door as he went.

Then he ran into Rick, and the chase was on.

Tyler puffed on his cigarette one last time and stubbed it out, even though it was only half-smoked. It joined a small pile of cigarette butts which had collected in the ashtray while he was telling Rick what had happened earlier in the dressing room that night.

Tyler reached for the pack on the table to shake out one more. There was only one left. "Last cigarette," he said, lighting up.

"Go ahead, take it," Rick said. Tyler blew smoke in his face.

"How much were you into the casinos for?" Rick asked.

"Enough. The people that set this up said if I dropped just this one, they'd square everything I owed. I didn't have a choice."

"You coulda declared bankruptcy."

"Be serious," the champ said—or was he no longer "the champ"? That would be a knotty one for the Boxing Commission to untangle.

"They didn't say what round they wanted it in, they were gonna let me know during the fight. There was a guy in the front row, acting drunk—he was supposed to give me the signal," Tyler said.

Rick sat back, head swimming. "A drunk—! That slob with the big red face?!"

Tyler went on as if he hadn't heard him. "They told me what he was gonna say, the words to listen for. That was how I was gonna know him, and it was gonna be the signal to go down. I ain't never gonna forget those words, never: 'Here comes the pain.'"

Rick nodded; it was all coming together now.

"That mouthy motherfucking piece of shit," Tyler said feelingly. "It was all I could do not to take *him* out. One punch. Push that radio right through the side of his head."

"Radio?"

"Yeah, you know, he had one of them things in his ear. Anyway, the fight started. Ruiz was hopping around like the chickenshit little punk that he is, talking shit at me. He stung me on the nose and I swung without thinking and damned near knocked him out. I was just trying to shut him up; I barely even tapped him and I almost won the fight.

"He did head-butt me, that was no lie. So much shit went wrong, it was like he was doing everything he could to fuck up the deal. Right after that, I got the signal. Quicker than I thought, only two minutes into the fight. Maybe they were getting nervous.

"I wasn't supposed to go down right away, they were real clear about that. I had to take a punch, fall back into a corner, then let him charge in and knock me out. Had to take a few seconds."

Rick said, "They wanted everybody up, on their feet. Distracted. *So they'd get a clear shot!*"

Tyler vented smoke. "'Here comes the pain'—corny motherfuckers. When I heard that, I went into my act. But that stupid, short-armed son of a bitch Ruiz didn't follow through on the punch. I was already making like he'd hung one on me and it was too far gone to stop, so I started falling backward. By the time I realized he didn't connect, I was already in the corner.

"Ruiz did what he had to do and I hit the mat, down. And that's all. I swear to God, I didn't know they was gonna kill nobody. I thought they was just after the money. Nobody was supposed to die. She never said nothing about that."

Rick battened down on that last. "She?"

"Atlantic City. I fucking hate it. I hope that storm blows this whole mister motherfucking town away," Tyler said.

"Who's 'she'?"

"The runner, the go-between. The one that came to me in the first place, told me I was going down. I never met nobody else. Just her."

Rick was hot on the scent now. "You get a name?"

"Yeah, name, address, phone number, serial number, she gave me some pictures of herself too, you want to see them? No, I didn't get her name," Tyler said.

"Do you remember anything unusual about her?"

"Apart from her fixing the fight, you mean? I don't know. Her hair, maybe."

Rick seized on that. "What about it?"

"It was red. I mean, bright red. Like it was on fire or something," Tyler said. "I'd like to set it on fire. Set her ass on fire, too."

TEN

When Julia came out of the stall, the ladies' room was still empty. She wore one of the clean stolen tee shirts and the satin baseball jacket over that. There wasn't anything she could do about the pants, but they had been only lightly spattered compared to her blouse. By wearing the T-shirt outside her pants, she was able to cover most of the telltale blood spots.

She stuffed her bloody garments into a trash can. She went to the sink and splashed some cold water on her face and washed her red-stained hands. She looked at herself in the mirror. She was white-faced, haggard, and looked ten years older than she had before the shooting had started.

She exited the ladies' room, and plunged into the human traffic streaming through the arena halls. The bloody clothes had been a red flag screaming "Arrest me!" Now that she had gotten rid of them, she could move among the crowds with slightly more confidence.

The question was, move where? The front entrance of the arena was effectively sealed off, as was the gateway to the neighboring casino. Still, in a building of this size, there must be an unguarded door somewhere. . . .

Time was against her. Slowly but surely, the police would filter the crowd out of the arena, after first checking each person out one by one. Now, there was safety in numbers, and she could lose herself in the crowd. As the hours passed, though, and the crowd thinned, the net would tighten around her. And there were worse things for her to worry about than the police.

She drifted with the flow, letting the human tide carry her through the winding corridors, not really paying attention to where she was. Up ahead, at a junction of halls, was a knot of blue-shirted guards, eyeing passersby.

She saw them before they saw her. She didn't even know if they were looking for her, but she had no intention of finding out. Nearby, on her left, was a tunnel mouth. She entered it, following it to its far end and emerging on the arena floor.

There were hundreds of people wandering around in the arena, or milling around the ringside murder site. The gawkers pressed as close to the scene as the police would let them, craning to see some blood on the floor.

Julia crossed the arena in the opposite direction, distancing herself from the scene. She felt nakedly exposed moving in plain sight in the cavernous open space. The good thing was that it was too big for the police and security forces to keep close on all the people in it. Plus, they had their hands full securing the crime scene and keeping back the people and the press.

At the opposite end of the arena from the death site, Julia climbed some stairs and went through a tunnel into a display area, a kind of exhibition hall. The exhibits showcased Powell Industries' high-tech excellence. There were life-sized models of the aerospace manufacturer's state-of-the-art air-to-air and surface-to-air missiles, rocket boosters, instrument packages and modules, and the like. Interspersed among them were plenty of photo posters and larger-than-life blowups of Gilbert Powell.

The exhibits were grouped in a horseshoe shape in the semicircular space, with a giant American flag hanging from ceiling to floor as a backdrop. The flag was as big as a theatrical stage curtain.

Julia lifted an edge, looking behind it. There were a few feet of open space between the flag and the wall behind it, and what looked like an unguarded door.

She heard voices approaching. She went behind the flag, hurrying to the door. She paused, gripping the handle—what if the door was wired to an alarm that would go off when it was opened?

And yet, the door might prove to be her escape route. She took the plunge, gripping the door's tubular bar handle in both hands, and pushed it open.

Blinding light and furious noise assaulted her, an overwhelming sensory impact. The door opened onto the casino floor.

She stepped through, the spring-hinged door closing automatically behind her. She stood with her back to the wall and tried to get her bearings.

Between the colored lights, sound, and motion, the casino was like the inside of a pinball machine, all lit up and pinging.

Details began to emerge from the blur. The blue-shirted guards were everywhere, walking the floor, threading the aisles between the banks of hundreds of slot machines, clustered by the doors where long lines of gamblers were waiting to get out.

The security here was tighter than in the arena. Worse, there were a lot less cops and a lot more blue-shirted guards. Definitely not the place for Julia to be.

She turned around to go back through the door into the arena exhibit hall. She reached reflexively for the door-knob and drew up short—there was none.

No doorknob, no handle, nothing. On the casino side, the door was a sheet of smooth blank metal plate.

Now she was trapped in the casino. Out of the frying pan and into . . . what?

ELEVEN

Rick had to laugh. The members of the press were already steamed at being unable to cover the big story the way they liked, and having to rely on periodic updates and carefully manicured handouts from the authorities' publicity spokesmen. But they'd really throw a fit when they found out about Lou Logan's monopoly on exclusive inside coverage.

Tough.

Lou was doing his thing right now, interviewing Dunne, of all people. Rick got a kick out of that. Call it When Worlds Collide.

A makeshift interview space had been set up in a corridor off the front lobby of the arena—a nice private alcove behind a blind corner, with security guards barring approaches to ensure that it stayed private.

Dunne stood in front of a camera, holding a document in one hand. Lou stood across from him, microphone in hand, doing his best imitation of a big-time network news anchorman. Rick wondered if Dunne knew who the hell Lou was.

The interview was being covered by a Powell PPV TV crew.

"We are now able to give you the identity of the assassin at this time," Dunne said, speaking for the record. He began reading from the paper he held.

"Tarik ben Rabat, thirty-seven years old, a Palestinian who has lived in the United States for the last six years. Mr. Rabat wrote a series of increasingly threatening letters to various congressmen expressing his outrage over the sale of U.S. missile systems and other weaponry to Israel. We had been tracking his whereabouts."

Dunne glanced up from the document and caught sight of Rick standing on the sidelines, off-camera.

"How many shots were fired in total?" Lou asked.

"There were three shots. Two from the assassin, one of which struck the secretary in the neck. He was taken to the Atlantic City Medical Center, but I have no information about his condition.

"My shot was the third, and it killed Mr. Rabat. That's all I can really say until the FBI joins the investigation shortly," Dunne said.

Lou tried to ask another question, but Dunne ignored him. A squad of blue shirts came trotting up the hall.

"That's it. Cut," Dunne told the cameraman. He crossed to the blue shirt's squad leader. "Did you find her?" Dunne asked.

"No."

"God *damn* it."

"She might have gone into the casino," the squad

leader said. "There's at least a dozen service doors from here to there. We couldn't watch all of them."

"Double the men you have at the casino exits," Dunne said.

Rick pulled him aside. He had urgent business and the clock was running. "I gotta talk to you, Kevin."

"Not here. The conference room," Dunne said.

The conference room was on the mezzanine level at the front of the arena, part of a cluster of administrative offices. It was an enormous room, dominated by a long table with a bunch of chairs around it. Not far from the head of the table stood another, smaller table that held a large architect's model of the Millennium casino hotel complex, including the planned mega-structure that would rise out of the renovated arena.

A large mural on one wall showed an idealized Atlantic City Boardwalk and seascape. On the wall opposite the head of the table was a barn-door-sized photo-portrait of Gilbert Powell. The plush wall-to-wall carpeting was the color of money.

At the room's far end, opposite the door, stood a floor-to-ceiling glass wall that fronted the Boardwalk, overlooking it from a few stories up. It was level with the electric globe ball at the top of the missile marquee. The drapes were closed, but the ghostly outline of the beacon lights could be seen shining through them. The rain couldn't be seen, but it kept up a fierce constant drumming against the glass.

Rick briefed Dunne, bringing him up to speed on what he had learned. Dunne wasn't thrilled, but listened anyway. When Rick got to the part about the drunk, Dunne broke in.

"How do you know it wasn't a hearing aid? Just because a guy has something plugged in his ear—"

"Tyler says it was a radio," Rick said.

"Yeah, great witness. Even if he's right, so what? What does it mean?"

"It means there was somebody on the other end, telling him what to do."

"Who cares? You just said Tyler threw the fight, what does it matter how they did it? I shouldn't have to tell you this, but guys throw fights all the time, it's got nothing to do with this."

"It's connected. It's all connected," Rick said stubbornly.

Dunne threw his hands up. "Oh, please. We got a file an inch thick on this guy Rabat, he's a well-known nutcase. This may be a tragedy, but it's no conspiracy."

"Tell me what really happened, Kevin."

"What?!" Dunne was taken aback.

"Right after the fight started. Where were you?"

"You already know. I saw the guy and I—"

"Not our bullshit. The truth."

Dunne looked at him like he was crazy. "What are you doing? Why are you chasing this like the world ends in ten minutes?"

Rick wasn't so sure of the answer himself. "Seems like the thing to do," he said, shrugging.

Dunne paced around in a circle on the rug, then came back to the table, where Rick was sitting perched on a corner.

Dunne said, "What do you care? You don't get out of bed unless there's an angle in it for you. . . . Uh-oh, wait a minute, now I got it. You think you're gonna get on TV and run for mayor. This is your big shot, right?"

"You finished?"

"I've got news for you, pal, in half an hour when the feds get here, you're Charlie Nobody and out the back door, the way you came in."

"The red-haired woman that you followed is the same person who told Tyler to throw the fight," Rick said. He held up his hand and counted off the points. "She's one. The shooter, he's two. Tyler is three. The drunk who shouted the signal is four. And whoever was on the other end of that radio is five.

"Five people make a conspiracy, and I'm chasing it because whoever set it up was probably smart enough to make sure that by the time the feds get here, all the loose ends are gonna be tied up nice and tight."

After a pause, Dunne said, "Whew! I hope you haven't told anyone else what you just told me."

"Why?"

"Because you sound like a fucking nut, that's why. What have you got? Hearsay from a compulsive gambler who admits he took a dive, and a mystery man and woman you can't get your hands on. Where's the objective evidence? You know how many conspiracy freaks like you come forward after an assassination?"

"Do you think I'm wrong?" Rick asked.

"Look at James Earl Ray, for Christ's sake. They got witnesses, a gun, and a confession, and most people *still* think he's not the guy."

"Kevin, you're too pissed off, it doesn't ring true. Look me in the eye and tell me: do you think I'm wrong?"

Dunne looked at him for a long time before saying, "No. I don't."

"So it's something else, then."

"That's right. It's something else. Something—personally embarrassing to me."

Dunne continued, "If it's at all possible, Rick, I'd be very grateful if what I'm about to tell you does not find its way into your report. If it's possible. I realize this calls for potentially unethical behavior on your part—"

"Oh, fuck all that shit, Kevin. Just tell me the Goddamn problem."

Dunne pulled out a chair on the right side of the table and sat down. He sat upright, back straight, feet on the floor, hands resting on the tops of his thighs. He was still, with no betraying nervous tics. His face was straight.

Rick pulled out a pack of cigarettes. Before the interview, he'd bummed a smoke off Lou Logan, then "forgotten" to return the pack. It wasn't his brand, but at least it was nicotine.

"Smoke?" he asked, offering one to Dunne. Dunne waved it off. "No, of course not," Rick said. "You don't smoke."

He fired one up and puffed smoke while Dunne started talking.

"That classified trip I mentioned before? It was a weapons test," Dunne began. "The AirGuard, Powell's new antimissile system, light years ahead of anything else. It delivers what the Patriot only promises. The tracking system can pick up an enemy missile as small as a baseball bat and vaporize it with a single missile fired from a jeep.

"Kirkland was ecstatic over the test, and by the time we got to the fight tonight, we were all high as kites. Kirkland's only been in office a few months and he wants to launch a reform movement. A successful new defense system is just what he needed to get some momentum."

He paused a moment, then said, "I lost my edge."

Now Dunne was a guy blaming himself for doing something stupid.

"Tell me about it," Rick responded.

It was the redhead. She didn't fit the pattern, Dunne told Rick. It's what he had told himself earlier, before the fight, when he had first spotted the redhead sitting across the aisle from him at ringside.

There were always a lot of beautiful women at ringside for the big fights, but it was more a case of them following the money rather than following the fights. They were almost always on the arms of guys who could afford to pop for the high-priced tickets, which could sometimes run a couple of thousand dollars each.

That was okay, that was part of the pattern. But the redhead sat alone, in one of the best seats in the house. It wasn't natural, it didn't fit the pattern. It irked him.

When the fight went off and Rick was watching the ring action, Dunne watched the redhead. All in the line of duty, of course. That's what he told himself. Or maybe he just wanted to eye a good-looking woman.

She caught him looking at her, smiled flirtatiously, and looked away. That's when Dunne said to Rick, "She's not even watching the fight."

Dunne got out of his seat, crossing the aisle to speak to the redhead. By so doing, he had unwittingly opened a sight line in front of the secretary, thanks to the empty chair.

The redhead knew he was standing beside her for a long time before she looked up at him, all wide-eyed and surprised, but pleasantly so.

"Hi, I'm Serena," she said. "What's your name?"

"Could I see your ticket, please?" Dunne asked.

"My what?"

"Your ticket, miss, I need to see your ticket for this seat."

"You don't look like an usher," she said, giggling. She started fiddling around inside her bag, obviously stalling. "I think I have it . . . somewhere," she said.

A burst of ring action brought a roar from the crowd, and Dunne looked to see what it was. While he was looking away, Serena hopped up and walked quickly away from him across the arena.

"Hey!" Dunne said, following her. Serena hurried up the steps toward the mouth of Tunnel 26. Dunne climbed after her, caught up, and looked up the stairs at the vision of her bewitching ass.

He trailed her into the tunnel. As he went in, he was passed by a blonde woman in a white suit who was going out. At the time, he barely noticed her.

He caught up with Serena in the tunnel, grabbing her by the arm and turning her around.

"Excuse me, miss. Where do you think you're going?"

"To the bathroom. Is that okay with you?"

"In the middle of the first round? Not much of a fight fan, are you."

She tried getting huffy. "Look, I don't know who you are, but you have no right to hassle me like this."

"Actually, I get paid to hassle," Dunne said. "Now drop the act and show me your ticket or I'll have you escorted out."

She dropped the bluster and tried wheedling, softening her tone to that of a pleading teenage girl. "Okay, I don't have a ticket. I mean, I have a ticket, but it's up in the nosebleed seats; I couldn't see anything. I do this all the

100

time, they always let me get away with it, it's no big deal."

"Tonight it is."

Somebody was walking toward them, through the tunnel. Another latecomer, a shaggy-haired bearded guy walking slowly with a stiff right leg.

Dunne also had something that was getting stiff, and it wasn't his leg. Serena leaned into him, just barely touching him. Her dress had a halter top and a plunging V-neck that bared the tops of her breasts almost down to the nipples. Her nipples were outlined against the fabric, bobbing a hairline away from his chest.

"What's so special about tonight?" Serena breathed, looking up at him with shiny brown eyes.

"There's a very important man in the crowd," Dunne said, his mouth suddenly dry.

The shaggy-haired guy walked by and continued on toward the arena end of the tunnel. Dunne barely gave him a glance, then returned his full attention to Serena.

"What're you, like, a bodyguard?" she asked.

"You might say that."

"That must be a very exciting job." She slid one leg forward, brushing a rounded thigh lightly against his crotch.

"It's got its moments," Dunne replied.

"How'd you like to guard . . . my body?" She pressed her breasts against his chest.

He looked around to see if anybody was watching, just in time to glimpse the shaggy-haired man down at the end of the tunnel pull a rifle from the baggy pants flopping around his stiff right leg.

Dunne tore away from Serena. The shaggy-haired

man, who was Rabat, shouldered his rifle and sighted down into the arena and fired. Twice.

"NOOOOO!" Dunne shouted, running down the tunnel toward Rabat, his gun drawn. Rabat whirled, trying to swing the rifle around, but Dunne shot first. The back of Rabat's skull exploded and he flopped to the cement floor.

Dunne raced up and stood over the still-twitching body. He looked down across the arena, at the fallen body of the secretary, and at the empty chair right in front of him, the chair where he, Dunne, should have been sitting.

He looked back the other way and the tunnel was empty. Serena was gone.

"And my career in the Defense Protective Service will be gone, too, if anybody finds out about this fuckup," Dunne said, concluding his story.

Emotionally drained, he sat slumping in his chair at the head of the conference table.

"If I'd stayed in position, I would have taken that bullet, you know I would have," he said.

"Sure," Rick said.

"I wish I had, I wish to Christ I was back in that chair right now, bleeding to death. I've been in the service since I was eighteen years old—"

"I know."

"—in the service since I was eighteen years old, and I never did anything like this. You think I didn't have opportunities? There's guys that fuck around on duty every day and it never comes back to them. I take my eye off the ball for five Goddamn seconds—*five seconds!* and the walls fall in."

Rick stood up and stretched. "I like you better. Golden Boy fucked up, like the rest of us humans. I like you better. Look, Kevin, you've been getting me out of trouble since I was twelve years old. I owe you one."

He took out a handkerchief and tossed it to Dunne. "You're sweating. Makes you look guilty."

Dunne took it and wiped his face. Rick said, "You want objective evidence, we'll find it. The redhead and the drunk, the guy who shouted the signal to Tyler—they may still be in the building somewhere."

Dunne stood up, clutching the handkerchief in one fist. It stuck out of the top of his hand like a flower.

"We have to be very careful now, Rick. You don't just pull a thread out of a conspiracy, you take the whole thing down or you don't touch it."

"So we take the whole thing down," Rick said.

"Sure. If we can't come up with either one of these people, we're going to keep this to ourselves, forever. I mean, take it to our graves. If we tell the wrong person before we have enough proof, we'll end up at the bottom of the ocean."

"Okay. We'll find 'em or we'll drop it."

"And that woman that was talking to the secretary just before the gunshots, I want her too," Dunne said.

"Why?"

"Maybe she's the sixth plotter. She got up and ran away after being shot. Innocent people don't usually do that. I'll look for her, you try to find the other two."

Rick noticed some brown smears on the handkerchief he had given to Dunne, where Dunne had wiped his face. "What the hell is that? Makeup?"

"Don't give me any shit, they made me put it on for the TV camera," Dunne said, embarrassed.

TWELVE

Rick and Dunne came out of the conference room and followed a corridor until they came to a fork that branched two ways. They halted.

Dunne said, "You'll never find anybody just walking around the arena. Get up to the casino surveillance room—they've got cameras covering every inch of the place."

"Yeah, all right, I know a guy up there," Rick said.

"Is there anybody you don't know?"

"How would I know?"

Rick took the right-hand path, Dunne took the left. Dunne followed the passage until it took another turn. When he had gone around the corner, he stopped. He leaned against the wall, breathing hard. He was still sweating. He remembered that he still had Rick's handkerchief. He mopped his face with it.

He checked his watch, cursing under his breath. He

started walking again down the bright chute-like corridor. After various zigzags of the branching, he came to a door marked NO ADMITTANCE. There was a card-key slot to the right of the door. Dunne looked around to make sure he was alone, then took a magnetic strip card from his cardcase and swiped it through the slot. The auto-lock opened, and he opened the door and went through it into what proved to be a maintenance level.

He was in the service area, the guts of the building. There were hydraulic pumps, power plants, junction boxes, pipes, conduits, and cables.

Dunne crossed a long, narrow high-ceilinged space where the distant ceiling lights shone through a tangle of catwalks and metal stairways, making web-like patterns of light and darkness on the painted concrete floor.

At the end of the gallery, there was a short passage on the left, then a longer, wider one on the right. At the end of these, he found himself in a hangar-like storage bay with a loading dock with metal overhead doors at one end.

Dunne stood there a moment, motionless. He heard voices coming from one side of the bay, from behind a pile of crates. He crossed to the sound, light-footed, being very quiet. As he neared the stack, he saw a plume of cigarette smoke rising from behind it.

He slowly circled the crates. On the other side, two people were standing around nervously. Serena and the drunk.

Dunne stood there watching them for a while before either of them noticed he was there. Serena saw him first, gave a little start, then recovered quickly. Not quickly enough to hide the start, though.

"*There* you are," she said, making it sound as if Dunne was late for a date with her. Which he was, in a way.

Zeitz, the name of the "drunk," flipped his cigarette butt to the floor and stomped on it. He grabbed his jacket off the top of a crate and pulled it on. He was stone-cold sober, had been all night. His face was still red, though.

"We should have been out of here eleven minutes ago," he said.

"We're temporarily off our timetable," Dunne said. "Not all the cops are turning exactly as predicted."

He started to wander around, and strolled over to a workbench on one side of the loading dock. He reached under its table, feeling for something. He tugged the item and pulled it free of the duct tape that had been holding it in place—it was a handheld portable communicator.

A walkie-talkie.

"We need to make an adjustment in our endgame," Dunne said. He set the dial on top of the handset and keyed the mike twice. After a pause, two sharp bursts of static came in reply.

Dunne said to the radio, "We have a flat. Take the spare out of the trunk."

"Copy," the radio said.

Dunne set the radio down on the workbench. He walked around aimlessly, hands in his pockets, looking around. The sliding metal bay doors were rippling like curtains from the force of the storm.

"What kind of adjustment? Everything went perfectly," Zeitz said. Even at normal speaking levels, his voice still had that raw needling tone.

"Not perfectly. Not perfectly at all," Dunne said, a little tremor in his voice. "A local cop made both of you."

"What?" Zeitz said.

Serena said, "How?"

"He did, that's all that matters," Dunne said. He turned his back to them and went back to the workbench to get the radio. His back still to them, he took a silencer out of one pocket and screwed it onto the barrel of his service revolver. He kept his hands low, so the other two couldn't see what he was doing.

Zeitz and Serena came toward him. "What are we going to do?" Serena asked.

"I told you. We're making an adjustment," Dunne said.

Zeitz said, "You mean zero out the cop, right? That's the only thing we can do."

"That's one option." Silencer in place, Dunne turned around, facing them. "This is the other."

Serena must have already been suspicious, because she was reaching into her bag for the small but lethal pistol that she kept there. Dunn shot her in the forehead at point-blank range.

The sound of the bullet hitting her was louder than the silenced report, which sounded something like a light-bulb being broken.

A red dot gaped in the middle of Serena's forehead. She crumpled, dead.

For once, Zeitz had nothing to say. He saved his breath for running, lunging toward the loading dock. Dunne pointed the weapon at him.

The silencer made that busted-lightbulb noise two more times, as Dunne put two into the back of Zeitz's legs, cutting them out from under him. Zeitz went down.

Dunne crossed over to him and lowered the gun. Zeitz was in shock, disoriented. Punchy. He grabbed Dunne's knees and started trying to pull himself up.

Dunne didn't like that so well. At this angle, Zeitz was so close that he ran the risk of shooting himself.

"Wait," Zeitz said.

"Let go of my leg."

"I'm shot."

"Not enough," Dunne said. He managed to shake Zeitz off his leg, and shot him one final time through the top of the skull. Zeitz stretched out on the floor, dead.

The loading bay doors shook under the wind and rain. Dunne stood in place for a minute, breathing hard, disturbed. He started to unscrew the silencer, but it was hot, burning his hand. He set the gun down on the workbench, and cursed.

"Sloppy. Sloppy," he muttered to himself.

Outside the bay doors came a sound that was not from the storm—the growl of a heavy engine being revved up.

Dunne went to the big metal garage doors and hit a button on the wall. The door in front of him started to open, its machinery grinding as the metal curtain was rolled up.

The storm immediately invaded the dock area, the wind-whipped rain driving in sideways. A small lake of water that had built up outside the door rushed inside, creating a small flood. Dunne tried to get away from it, but the water was too quick, and sheeted across the floor, soaking his shoes.

"Goddamn it!" he exclaimed. He stepped back, his face disgusted as he shook the water off his shoes. A panel truck that had been waiting outside the door now rolled through it, into the bay of the loading dock.

Two men got out of the cab, leaving the motor running. They were the two security agents who were part of the secretary's detail, the two who had braced

Rick at ringside earlier tonight, before Dunne had cleared him.

They looked at Dunne, then at Serena and Zeitz dead on the floor. "Do I have to draw you a picture?" Dunne said.

Without a word, the two got to work, throwing open the rear doors of the truck and removing tarps and ropes and other needful items. Dunne took a towel from one of them and sat down on a wooden stool to wipe his shoes. They were soaked through to the socks. He wiped the water off, then blotted it with the towel. Every time he stepped down on one of the shoes, water squished out of it.

He tried polishing the shoes with the towel. "Fucking seawater. You know the kind of marks this leaves? Saltwater stains don't ever come out. This is the finest hand-stitched Italian leather. You know how much these shoes cost?"

The two agents opened up a tarp and spread it out between the corpses. They picked up Serena's body— one holding it by the ankles, the other by the wrists— and put it on one side of the tarp.

When they let go of the body, it rolled on its side, so that one of the arms was stretched out off the tarp and on the floor. On Serena's finger was a distinctive green stone ring. It matched her eyes, which were still open.

One of the agents picked up her arm by the wrist, repositioning it so that it lay alongside her on the tarp. He didn't bother to close her eyes.

Dunne was still working on his shoes. There was something obsessive about it. He kept rubbing them harder.

"Decaying. This entire situation. Circling the drain," he said.

The agent who hadn't repositioned Serena's arm found her bag and put it on the tarp beside her.

"The radio," Dunne said, interrupting his shoe fetish long enough to indicate the handset on the workbench.

The radio was placed on the tarp. The agents stood at the corners, ready for the wrap-up.

"Wait," Dunne said, unscrewing the silencer from his gun. He used Rick's handkerchief to wipe it clean of fingerprints, then dropped both onto the tarp.

His gun, the murder weapon, could tie him to two kills. Two kills, committed with his service revolver! The smart thing would be to toss the gun onto the tarp, too.

But it was the only gun he was carrying, and he wouldn't go without a gun. The night was far from over, and he wasn't out of the woods yet, not by a long shot.

Bodies, belongings—even the towels that had been used to mop up the blood from the floor, all went onto the tarp. All except the towel, which Dunne was still using to fuss with his shoes.

The agents rolled up the tarp, sealing it at both ends and in the middle with lengths of rope. They each took an end and hefted it. The tarp hung down like a hammock, one with two bodies in it.

They went out the bay door, into the storm. Not far from the loading dock, there was a construction site, part of the Millennium earthworks still in progress. It was a giant concrete caster used to make pillars for a planned colonnade. Parked beside it on a gravel lot was a large cement mixing truck, its lights dark, but its massive mixing barrel turning in the rain.

A hose plugged into the back of the truck led up to a

slide at the lip of a giant cast, a tall column in the shape of one of Powell's heavy-thrust booster missiles. Standing near the cast was a titanic cement missile that had already been cast and completed.

The agents slogged up a short walkway, carrying the swinging burden of the tarp between them, and wrestled it to the mouth of the steel cast.

The agents upended the tarp, over the lip of the cast. The bodies slithered out and tumbled into the cast, followed by the tarp. One of the agents threw a lever, switching on the flow. The pour-hose jumped, swelling like a garden hose when the water is turned on. A heavy stream of cement spurted from the fan-shaped nozzle, spewing, flowing down the slide, filling the steel cast and entombing the bodies.

A freak storm sent lightning crackling, thrusting jagged trident bolts across the sky, which was immediately followed by a crack of thunder. Then the sky went black.

The storm raged on. Ignoring it, Dunne kept polishing his shoes.

"Ruined," he said.

Ex-champs don't have many friends. Tyler was in his dressing room, alone, packing a gym bag. The door opened and Dunne came in.

Tyler looked at him, but Dunne was silent.

"What do you want?" Tyler asked.

THIRTEEN

The head of the Casino Surveillance Center was Walt McGahn, a squat ex-Atlantic City cop, a buddy of Rick's. He led Rick into the cockpit of the center, a small room that was packed with banks of video monitors, tiers of them. Three watchers sat at computer consoles, a dozen screens at each monitoring station.

The cameras seemed to give complete coverage of every nook and cranny of the casino hotel—tables, slots, lobby, restaurants, washrooms, corridors, elevators—everything but the guest rooms. And Rick wouldn't have been surprised if McGahn was able to peek into them, too. If he could, he was keeping it to himself.

"We've got fifteen hundred cameras, eight hundred on the casino side, seven hundred twenty on the hotel side, quadruple redundancy on the gaming floor. If they're down there, we'll find 'em."

"I appreciate it, Walt," Rick said.

McGahn motioned Rick to a chair at one of the watcher consoles. Rick slid into it.

"You think one of these people's your shooter, Rick?"

"We already got the shooter."

"Then what are you looking for?"

Rick just grinned. "I can take a hint," McGahn said. He pulled a keyboard around so that it faced him. "You tell me," he said.

"Lobby?"

"One eighteen." McGahn input the three-digit number into a keypad and a black-and-white image of the hotel lobby came up. Rick pulled up his chair and stared at the screen.

"Can you go to the right?" he asked.

"One fifty-four." McGahn typed in that number and the image switched over to another camera, covering the right side of the lobby.

"Keep moving, let's go by section," Rick said. Walt typed in another number, and the image changed to a shot just entering the casino.

"Keep going."

Walt keyed another number, and now they were into the slot machines, in rows, big blocks of them.

"No," Rick said.

But Walt stopped anyway, staring at a guy who was walking down a row of slots. "Hey, C.J., punch up three eighty-three. Guy in the Knicks shirt."

"What about him?" Rick asked.

"Coin-cup grabber." He said it as though it was one of the lowest, most loathsome crimes imaginable.

"The dirty bastard," Rick said. "You know him?"

"Nah. But that's how I make him. You get pretty good at reading the body language," McGahn said.

C.J., a young guy in his mid-twenties, punched up the camera on his monitor. "I got him."

McGahn and Rick looked at him, away from their own screen, which now showed the figure of a woman crossing between two of the rows of slots. It was Julia.

She stopped, looked around, her face in full, clear view of the camera for a moment. But Rick was looking at McGahn and C.J.

McGahn was expounding, "Somebody wants to play the slots, they look at the machines, trying to guess which one's lucky. Grabbers couldn't care less, they check out the people. They're like pickpockets, but crude. No skills."

Julia turned, so her back was to the camera when Rick and McGahn turned back to that monitor.

"Keep going?" McGahn asked.

"Keep going."

Julia had to keep going, as if she had a purpose down there on the casino floor. People are less likely to interfere with someone who looks like she knows what she's doing. She wished she *did* know what she was doing.

It was hard to concentrate out on the floor. Banks of hundreds of slots on all sides, their lights flashing, internal mechanisms jingling, bells ringing when they paid off—it was almost a physical assault on the senses.

She saw a bar area and changed course suddenly, veering toward it. A person who wandered toward the bar, or away from it, attracted little notice on the floor, unless he or she was becoming a nuisance. Anyone interfering even a little bit with the gambling was considered a prime nuisance, to be dealt with swiftly by the guards.

Julia didn't see any guards in the bar area. Another reason to go there. Besides, she needed to stop running and sit down and think, if only for a minute.

The bar area was on a raised platform at the edge of the casino floor. There was a curved wooden bar and some tables and chairs. On the other side of the platform, opposite the bar, was a stand where a lounge trio was doing a set. They weren't very good, but at least they didn't play too loudly.

Julia went in and looked around. A bank of big-screen TVs hung suspended from an overhead brace above the bar. They were mostly tuned into sports shows, but one of them was airing a special news report on the Kirkland assassination. On came a replay of the tape of Dunne's statement to Lou Logan.

Julia pressed in closer and edged toward the bar, unable to look at anything but the screen as she listened to Dunne talk and stared at his face.

Then the image cut to a photograph of Rabat, shaggy-haired, glum, with a ropelike mustache. A printed title underneath his picture identified him as "alleged assassin."

Julia thought that she might be sick. She put a hand to her mouth, gasping, openly dismayed.

A guy sitting nearby on a stool alone at the bar glanced at her, then brightened. He was about thirty, decent-looking, with a nice-enough face. Misunderstanding her reaction to the TV, he said, "Down on the game?"

She looked at him, confused, her mind blank. He gestured to a baseball game on another TV.

Julia got the concept. "Oh. Yeah. Yes. I'm down. Definitely."

116

Across from her at the tables, she could see a young couple nuzzling and getting amorous. She glanced sideways at the guy on the barstool, unconsciously adjusting her outfit.

"Uh . . . what's the score now?" she said, too brightly.

He didn't think it was unsubtle. He turned to face her. "Five–one Phillies in the eighth," he said.

"Oh. Oh. I'm not down, I'm dead," she said. "So . . . are you staying in the hotel?" She tried for a conversational tone, but it was a little forced.

"Yeah." He eyed her, noticing the curves of her high, firm breasts where she had unzipped her jacket enough to show them off. He took a sip of his drink, and then put his hands under the bar and tried to be discreet about taking off his gold wedding band and slipping it into his pocket.

That done, he said, "I'm Ned Campbell. Would you like to sit down?"

The video dragnet continued up in the surveillance room, images of the casino flashing and flickering on the screens, some in color, others in black and white. Blackjack tables, craps, roulette, men's room, ladies' room, more blackjack. Rick sat beside McGhan at the console, bleary-eyed and dizzy.

C.J. called out, "Walter, I think we've got another hooker in the Terminal Lounge."

"What, another?"

"The storm's bringing them out," somebody said.

"Bringing them in, you mean," said somebody else.

"Punch up five ninety-six, Walter," C.J. said.

"'Scuse me for a second," Walt said to Rick. Rick was

glad for the rest. He sat back in the chair and rubbed his eyes. Somewhere back between them, there was a thick knot of tension, and it was growing.

McGahn punched in five ninety-six, calling up the video image of a color shot of the lounge's bar area. Julia and Ned were cozying it up on a pair of bar stools. She sat very close to him, almost in his lap, where her hand was hovering. Instead she rested it on his thigh, and kept her other hand around his neck, playing with his hair. On the bar in front of them were a couple of drinks. Hers was practically untouched.

Julia leaned in and whispered something in his ear.

"She just got in there five minutes ago and she can't take her hands off him," C.J. said.

Rick stopped rubbing his eyes and took a look, mildly curious. What he saw was electrifying.

"Holy Christ, that's her!"

As if spooked by Rick's shout, the video images of Julia and Ned got up to leave.

"You said she had red hair," McGahn said accusingly.

Rick jumped up. "No, not that one, somebody else. Where's that bar? Shit, they're leaving!"

On the screen, Ned pulled out his wallet to pay for the drinks and put a twenty on the bar.

"No problem, I'll stay with 'em," McGahn said.

"I gotta get down there, where is it?"

McGahn took down two handset radios from a rack and tossed one to Rick, who snagged it out of the air on his way to the door. "Stay on channel three," McGahn said.

On the monitor, Ned was pocketing his change. He took Julia by the hand and they walked off, out of camera range.

Rick was out the door.

FOURTEEN

Now the net was closing tighter, faster.

Julia and Ned crossed the casino floor, moving toward the elevators. A blue-shirt security guard spotted her from across a row of tables and came to an abrupt halt. He nudged his partner, who also saw her and radioed in a report.

The report did not go to McGahn's Casino Surveillance Center.

Rick burst out of a door marked AUTHORIZED PERSONNEL ONLY, and found himself at the edge of the vast casino floor. He radioed McGahn, saying, "I'm on the floor. Where is she?"

In the surveillance room, C.J. punched buttons, tracking Julia and Ned through the casino. McGahn had Rick on his monitor.

"You're on the opposite side of the room. They're

walking past the slots near the far elevators," McGahn radioed back.

Ned stopped at a slot machine and fed a coin into it.

"What are you doing?" Julia asked.

"Hang on, I just want to play this change. I don't like having a lot of loose change cluttering up my pockets," he said.

He pulled the arm, and the wheels started spinning. Over the top of the machine, Julia saw two blue-shirt guards heading her way, closing in.

"I want to go upstairs," she said, very definitely.

The machine hit, and spit five dollars' worth of quarters into the coin till like rivets while the balls went *ding ding ding ding!*

"I won!" Ned cried.

"Let's go upstairs. Maybe you'll get lucky again," she said. The blue-shirted duo was closer. Ned started scooping up the coins from the till.

"I want to go upstairs now," Julia said. "If you don't want to come, I'm sure someone else will." She turned and walked off, quickly.

Ned picked up the last of the coins and stuffed them in his pants pocket, then ran after her. "Hey, wait. . . ."

Dunne burst out a door and onto the casino floor, closing with the two blue-shirts, the ones who had first seen Julia.

"They said you spotted her?" Dunne said.

One of the guards pointed. "Over there, headed toward the elevators."

"Good job! I got it from here." Dunne stepped off, heading toward Julia and Ned in the distance.

Rick wasn't having as much luck. He weaved in and

out of the blocks of slots, searching but not finding. "They're not here, Walt, they're not here!"

McGahn radioed back, "Change of plans! We just picked them up again. They're at the elevators. Ten yards ahead of you and turn right."

An elevator touched down on the floor, the doors sprang open, and Julia and Ned climbed in.

A second later, Dunne got on board. Julia stared at him, afraid. Ned was oblivious. He started to reach up for the elevator buttons, but before he could, she put a hand on his arm, stopping him.

"What floor?" she asked Dunne, her voice brittle.

Dunne raised an eyebrow and looked at her for a long pause before saying, "Twenty-one."

She pushed it for him, and the button lit up. She made no move to push a button of her own.

"Same for you?" Dunne asked pleasantly.

Ned pulled his hand free of hers and jabbed thirty-five. "Thirty-five, actually," he said, slipping his arm possessively around Julia's waist. She closed her eyes as the doors closed and the elevator started up.

The elevator doors closed right in Rick's face, just before he could get a foot inside the car. Rick had arrived a second too late, but in time to see Julia standing leaning in the corner of the elevator, eyes shut. He had seen Ned, too.

Had he been standing at a different angle, he would have seen Dunne, but his buddy was hidden behind the already closing door. Dunne didn't see him, either.

When he had stopped pounding the wall in frustration, Rick used the radio. "Missed it! You got 'em in the elevator car?"

The cameras had them, with a view mounted in a front

corner of the elevator car's ceiling, facing down at the riders.

Dunne, Julia, and Ned.

"Got 'em. Them and one other guy," McGahn said.

"What floor are they going to?"

"Can't make out the buttons . . . it's a high one, though."

"Can you pick 'em up when they get off? I gotta know what floor!"

"I'd have to look floor by floor, I'd miss 'em. Hang on, I got an idea," McGahn said.

He shoved back in his wheeled swivel chair and rolled up to the first monitor he had worked for Rick earlier. He hit the rewind button and the surveillance tape zapped back to when Julia and Ned were in the bar.

Back in the elevator, the car stopped on the twenty-first floor and the doors bounced open. Dunne made no move to get off.

"This is twenty-one," Ned said helpfully.

Smiling with his lips, nodding, Dunne stepped off and stared at Julia as the doors closed in front of him. He punched the "up" button for another elevator.

Alone with Julia in the elevator, Ned turned to her, wrapped his arms around, and kissed her on the mouth. With tongue. Julia kissed back a little, faking it as best she could. His mouth was wet, warm, clumsy.

He was still kissing her when the car stopped on thirty-five. She stepped back, breaking the clinch. "We'd better go to your room," she said.

"Couldn't agree more."

They stepped off the elevator and started down the hall.

McGahn had had a good look at Ned when he had

been back at the bar, captured on videotape at the moment that he was paying for his drinks. McGahn squinted for a few seconds at the video image of Ned holding up his wallet.

"Ooh, baby, right there," he said. He froze the image and punched in a command. The image zoomed in, way in, on Ned's wallet. His driver's license was visible in a little picture window in one flap. McGahn rode the zoom down into it, expanding the detail until the name and address on the card were legible. He locked it in, then reached for a phone and called the hotel's front desk.

"This is McGahn in security. We have a Ned Campbell staying in the hotel? . . . Yes? What room?"

Next, McGahn radioed to Rick, "Room 3517."

"You're a genius," Rick said. He could have kissed the radio. Instead, he hit the button for another elevator.

"This is where I lose you, Ricky. Watch your back." McGahn signed off.

Dunne bounced out of the elevator on the thirty-fifth floor, ready for a showdown. But Julia and Ned were nowhere in sight. The elevators were in the middle of a long corridor, empty except for Dunne.

On impulse, Dunne went to the right, double-timing it, not really running, but jogging. The loose change and keys in his pants pockets jingled merrily as he went to the end of the corridor, which opened onto another hallway that met it at right angles, forming a "T."

The right-hand branch was empty, but at the end of the left-hand branch, two figures were just rounding the corner, moving out of sight. It was a long way off and Dunne wasn't exactly sure it was them, but he went after them anyway.

The corridor seemed endless, a carpeted tube lined on both sides by closed doors. Finally he was near the far end, and Dunne slowed, then looked over his shoulder to make sure he was alone. He was.

He drew his weapon and sprang the clip, checking it. After Serena and Zeitz, he still had half a clip yet. And those two were pros. This would be enough for what he had to do. He fed the clip into the slot at the butt of the grip, then smacked it with the heel of his palm to make sure it was properly seated. He didn't have to jack a round into the chamber; one was already there.

He reached across his belly and held the gun under his jacket flap, which hid it from casual detection. He came abreast of the corner, took a deep breath, stepped into the next hallway. . . .

Empty. But Julia and Ned had gone in this direction, he was sure of it. So—where did they go? Around the next corner, or into one of the rooms along the way?

He raced all the way down the length of the corridor, and looked around the corner. No luck. But they couldn't have gotten this far in such a short time, so they had to have gone into one of the rooms along this corridor; and not too very deep into it, either. Again, there wasn't time for them to have gotten much farther. They had to be in one of the rooms in the lower half of the corridor. That narrowed the search.

He turned, retracing his steps to the start of the hallway. He stood against the first door on his right, listening. The quarry had gone to cover, and he had to pick up the scent.

Inside the room, voices, a man's and a woman's, were arguing with the rancor that only comes from a long, unhappy marriage. She was lacing into him for dropping too much money at the tables, while he was throwing her drinking problem back at her.

Dunne crossed the hallway to stand at the door on the left. He listened for some sounds from inside that room, something, anything to tell him whether the trail was getting hotter or colder.

An operation of this magnitude, and he was reduced to this, listening at doors and keyhole-peeping, like a snoopy hotel detective. Still, sometimes the old ways were the best.

Like the way he had handled Serena and Zeitz.

In his room, Ned Campbell was busy getting into the mood for love. First, though, he switched on the TV. It was almost time for the sports news to come on. There were a couple of teams he was following, and he wanted to see how they had done in tonight's games. Maybe it wasn't the most romantic ploy ever, but Julia was in the bathroom anyway. When she came out, he'd turn it off. Then he'd turn her on. Yeeoww!

In his shaving kit, he had a little bottle of breath freshener, which he always took with him on the road. He was a representative for a company that manufactured plastic cup holders, and his job required him to do a lot of selling. He was in town on a sales trip—his company did a lot of business with the casino hotels. His business was done, but there was no leaving town, not in this storm. So tonight he was staying over, and it was fun time! The weather gave him a legitimate excuse for not going home, and he'd already squared the overnight with his wife when he'd talked to her earlier over the phone. It'd be just like her to call the hotel again to check up on him. He thought of telling the desk to hold all calls, but that wouldn't do; it would only make her suspicious. Aw, to hell with her. If she called, he'd think of some way to get rid of her fast.

He spritzed some breath-freshening spray into his open mouth. He used the stuff a lot on the job. You can't sell if you're worried about your breath offending the clients. Or the ladies.

He glanced at the bathroom door, wondering how Julia was coming along, what she was doing in there. Getting ready for sex? Putting in a diaphragm or something . . . That brought up the worrisome question of safe sex. Needless to say, he wasn't the type to go around packing a few condoms, just in case. If his wife ever caught him with one of those, she'd be sure he was fucking around, she'd tear his cock off.

Ned giggled. He *was* fucking around. That'd show her! As for the condoms, well, maybe Julia had some. He'd heard that some women did that. Or seen it on TV, anyway. He'd been married so long that he didn't know what a single woman did anymore. Anyway, he was sure she'd have something to protect herself. It was the woman's responsibility; she was the one who could get pregnant.

Thinking of his wife gave Ned a start. *His wedding ring!* Panic seized him until he remembered which pocket he'd put the ring into, and found it there. He'd been a little sloshed in the bar, and it made him a bit careless. If he lost his wedding band, he'd never be able to explain that away.

He took out his wallet and put the gold band carefully in a little pocket with a snap-on flap, where it would be safe.

On TV, the weatherman was giving an update on the storm:

". . . upgraded Jezebel to a level two, with wind speeds between 96 and 110 miles per hour. If and when a level two hurricane makes landfall, you're looking at a storm surge of up to fifteen feet, which would result in flooding—"

Click! Ned switched channels with the remote. Where were those sports scores? Before he could switch channels again, a "Special Bulletin" graphic flashed on the screen.

A new reader came on, saying, "Once again updating our breaking story, Secretary of Defense Charles Kirkland is in critical condition at the Atlantic City Medical Center after being struck by an assassin's bullet while attending a boxing match at the Atlantic City Arena."

The shooting had taken place virtually next door. That'd give Ned something to tell the folks back home. He eyed the bathroom door, behind which came the sound of running water. He'd have something to tell his buddies back home, too. The pity was, they'd never believe him.

On the screen, the announcer went on. "We've been getting live updates from the only reporter allowed inside the arena, a Lou Logan of Powell Pay-Per-View Television. We're going to be going live with him now. . . .

"Sorry, I've just been informed that there'll be a slight delay before bringing you that exclusive report from inside Atlantic City Arena, where earlier tonight . . ."

Ned held his wallet in his hand, wondering what to do with it. He assumed he was getting a free ride. Julia was no hooker, of that he was sure. Hookers never went up to the room without first settling on the price. He'd never

127

been with a hooker, but that's what he'd heard. But she'd never mentioned money, and if she didn't, he sure wouldn't. Not that he wouldn't be willing to spend a little if he had to, but if it was free, so much the better.

Besides, she didn't dress or act like a hooker. Hookers looked a lot sexier than that. Not that she didn't have a sexy little bod, what'd he'd seen of it through her jacket and T-shirt. She filled out those white pants nicely with a cute little behind.

Still, why take chances? Ned had his credit cards and a couple hundred bucks in cash in his wallet. He hid it in the back of his suitcase, among the rolled socks.

He found a couple of beer-bottle-sized bottles of champagne in the mini-bar, and set them out on a round lamp-table. He went around the room and turned off some of the lights to make the mood more romantic.

In the bathroom, Julia was stripped from the waist up, except for her bra. The top half of the manila envelope showed where it stuck out of the top of her pants, against her flat tummy. The makeshift bandages lay on top of the toilet tank, with the folded T-shirt that she'd used for a pad soaked with dried blood.

She examined her wound in the mirror. The bleeding seemed to have stopped, clotting up in the dark furrow that marred her pinkish-white flesh. A massive purple-brown bruise was swelling up on the injured shoulder.

It felt like the gouge had been grooved by a hot curling iron. The tear was about the same thickness as an iron, but was luckily shallow.

She noticed a bottle of Advil on the sink counter, grouped with some complimentary bottles of shampoo and bars of soap from the hotel. She shook four tablets into her hand and swallowed them down with a glassful of water from the sink. She stuffed another dozen into her pants pocket for later. If there was a later.

One of Ned's dress shirts hung on a hook on the bathroom door. She reached for it, hearing something on the TV that made her pause and listen closely. It was loud enough that she could hear it through the closed door.

". . . take you now to Lou Logan of Powell Pay-Per-View Television, coming to you live from Atlantic City Arena, where Secretary of Defense Charles Kirkland was critically wounded earlier tonight in an apparent assassination attempt," the network newsreader said.

Julia stood with her ear pressed to the door, to hear better.

"Mr. Logan? Lou Logan, are you there? Mr. Logan, what can you tell us about the status of the investigation into the shooting of Secretary Kirkland at this time?"

Lou Logan came on, parroting the feed he'd gotten earlier from Dunne. "The assassin has been identified as one Tarik ben Rabat, a Palestinian terrorist with ties to the Hamas and Hezbollah extremist factions. Rabat has been living in the United States, where he has a history of serious mental illness and writing threatening letters to government officials.

"Rabat was killed immediately after the shooting by a member of Secretary Kirkland's security detail. The agent had reportedly noticed Rabat in the crowd acting suspiciously, and went to investigate, when—"

Click!

Ned had gotten restless and changed channels, and a new voice was sounding on the TV:

". . . it was a big night for the Phillies on their West Coast road trip, as they racked up an impressive five–one win against their opponents, the hard-charging . . ."

129

There was more, but Julia didn't hear it. She stood with her back to the door, fists clenched, thinking hard, wondering what her next move would be.

Outside, in a different context, Ned was wondering the same thing.

FIFTEEN

Julia came out of the bathroom wearing Ned's shirt over her pants. The top buttons were fastened so that only a small V of pinkish-white flesh at the top of her chest showed. But under the baggy shirt, her figure was trim and appealing.

"I was starting to worry about you, I thought you fell in," Ned said.

"Ha, ha," Julia said. "I hope you don't mind, I borrowed your shirt."

"Not at all. You look better in it than I do." He went over to her and slipped his arms around her slim waist, pulling her close to him. Her body was taut, athletic, but with nicely rounded curves.

"I think women look sexy in men's shirts," he murmured, "and even sexier without them." He had her in a clinch, and bent his head to kiss her.

His breath was warm and smelled of breath freshener.

He put his mouth on hers, covering it. His tongue pressed against her closed lips. Reluctantly, she opened her mouth, and he shoved his tongue in it.

A professional would have known how to handle the situation, but Julia was only an amateur in a deadly game where the pros played for keeps. The kissing she could tolerate, in a kind of nauseated apathy, but when he reached down behind her and put his hands on her buttocks, feeling and squeezing them through her pants, she'd had enough.

She broke out of the kiss, gasping. "Just—hold on a minute."

"Huh?!"

She slithered out of his arms, breaking the clinch. Dazed, she dropped into a sitting position on the bed.

Ned looked down at her, at the top of her head. Her face was level with his crotch, and he couldn't believe his luck. He figured this cute little babe was set to give him some oral action, some head royale. The guys back home would never believe it.

He unbuckled his belt and started unzipping the top of his pants. When Julia realized what he was doing, she jumped up, revolted, and pushed past him.

"Not *that*," she said, shuddering.

Ned was offended. "Well, excuuuuuuuse me."

"Can't you get out of my face for just one minute?"

"Hey, you're the one who was practically giving me a hand job down in the bar."

Julia forced herself to be calm. "Let's start again. I need a place where I can just—wait. A little bit. And then I'll go."

"Wait a little bit? And then you'll go? What do you think this is, a bus station?"

Outside, in the hall, creeping around from door to door, Dunne caught part of Ned's outburst coming from a room, muffled by walls. Too muffled for him to recognize Ned's voice, which he had heard in the elevator.

It didn't mean anything to Dunne, so he kept on moving, prowling outside the next door.

In Ned's room, the scene was getting ugly, as was Ned, who now saw all his dreams of hot fantasy sex with a strange broad in his hotel room going out the window.

"Would you keep your voice down?" Julia pleaded.

"Are you on drugs or something? Yeah, you look like hell, I should have been able to figure that one out. Thought you were gonna get me up here and rob me, is that what you thought?"

Julia tried the truth, always a losing proposition. "I'm in trouble. Someone is trying to kill me—"

"Oh Christ, now I've heard it all."

"Please, listen to me, haven't you heard anything about what happened tonight?"

He pointed to the door. "Just get out, will you? I'm a happily married man, and I don't need your kind of trouble."

"Half an hour, that's all I'm asking."

"Get out."

"Please, I'm begging you—"

"I said *get out*." He grabbed her by the arm and pushed her toward the door.

Julia wailed, "No, wait, please . . ."

He tore the locks open, flung open the door, and shoved her out the doorway, directly into the arms of—

Rick.

Julia took one look at him and opened her mouth to

scream, but Rick covered her mouth with his hand and pushed her back into the room, forcing Ned to give ground and step aside.

Rick heeled the door behind him shut. He began, "It's all right—"

"Who the hell are you?" Ned burst in.

"Take a walk, will ya?"

"What the fuck is going on around here?!"

"I said—" Rick grabbed Ned by the shoulder, opened the door, and flung him through it, into the hall.

"—take a fucking walk," Rick finished, slamming the door shut.

Ned stood out on the hallway, staring open-mouthed at his room door. He tried the knob. It was locked. He rattled it, but it stayed locked. He felt around in his pockets for his room key, remembering that he'd left it inside, on top of the bureau. His wallet was inside, too.

He started pounding on the door, shouting, "It's *my* fucking room!"

Atlantic City casino hotel doors are nice and solid, and Ned couldn't make a dent in it. On the other side of the door, Rick badged Julia, holding out his photo ID so she could see he was who he said he was. She stood a healthy distance away from him, less panicked now that he had let go of her, but still wary and alert.

"Remember me? You sat next to me at ringside," he said.

After a pause, she nodded. "Please help me, I've got to get out of the building."

Ned got tired of his futile pounding on the door and walked away, ranting as he stalked off down the corridor.

"You sure know how to piss a guy off," Rick said.

Ned was heading for the elevators, sounding off at the

top of his lungs, when he met Dunne coming the other way. Ned shut up when he saw Dunne barreling toward him. Dunne's weapon was once more safely hidden away in his shoulder holster, or Ned would really have been struck speechless.

"Hotel Security," Dunne said. "Where is she?"

"That wacko broad locked herself in my room! She—"

"Give me the key," Dunne said, holding out his hand.

"I don't have it, it's in the room!"

"What room?"

"3517."

"It's not the first time she's tried to pull this," Dunne said. "She's a shakedown artist who works the hotels. We'll try to keep you out of it, the hotel doesn't want any bad publicity, either. Go down to the bar for an hour or two and we'll get this taken care of quietly."

"Thanks, I'd appreciate it. If my wife . . ."

But Dunne was already striding away. "Hey!" Ned called after him, "There's a guy in the room with her."

Dunne stopped short and looked back. "What guy?"

"A tough guy, a real mean prick. I figure he's her pimp or something."

"Right. Okay, get lost."

Ned didn't have to be told twice. He moved out toward the elevators, fast.

Dunne halted outside Room 3517. He could hear a TV going inside. Cautiously, with a very light touch, he tried the doorknob, but it was locked.

No time to play it smooth, he had to bust in, and these doors didn't give too easily. He drew his gun and fired one into the lock, blowing it away. The shot was louder than hell, but that would surprise them inside, paralyze them for a few critical split seconds.

The door flew open from the force of the blast. Dunne charged inside, holding the gun out in front of him with both hands, in a combat shooting stance.

But the room was empty. Julia and friend were gone.

SIXTEEN

Rick took Julia through a fire door, into a stairwell. She started to go downstairs, but Rick grabbed her arm, saying, "No, up."

They climbed one flight, two flights, three flights, and then they ran out of stairs. Above them was nothing but a square-sided ceiling, unbroken by any hatch or access door. A vertical dead end.

Julia couldn't have climbed any more, she was exhausted, panting. "This is good," Rick said.

"No! We can't stop in here!" Julia said.

Rick pointed upward to the ceiling's four empty corners. "No cameras. We're alone, for a minute. Come on, sit down before you fall down."

She sat down on the top step, shaking. He sat beside her. He shook two cigarettes out of the pack and offered her one. She took it, her hand shaking as she put it to her lips. He steadied her hand, giving her a light.

"Thank you." She took a puff and exhaled, then started to cry. Her head bowed and her shoulders shook as she made liquid noises. Rick squirmed, uncomfortable. He patted her on the back, a little awkwardly. "Shh, shh. You're safe now," he said.

After she had quieted down some, he asked, "Why did you run away?"

"I don't know. I don't know what I'm doing," she said.

"One thing you can do is stop crying and tell me what you know."

She looked at him, measuring, weighing. After a pause, she pulled up the tails of her shirt—Ned's shirt, actually—and pulled the manila envelope out of the top of her pants.

"What's that?" Rick asked.

Julia took a deep breath. "I work at Powell Aircraft. I put together the ballistics reports we issue after weapons tests."

"Like the one they had for the new missile? The whatchamacallit, the AirGuard?"

She glanced at him sharply, suspicious. "You know about that?"

"The name came up, that's all."

"The AirGuard, yeah. For the past couple of months, I've suspected that the reports we're issuing on the AirGuard were doctored. I sent anonymous E-mail messages to Secretary Kirkland, warning him. I was afraid to call him or go there in person, I didn't know who I could trust. He E-mailed me back and told me to get him proof," she said. "Yesterday, I got this."

She held up the envelope, wrinkled, frayed, and streaked with her blood. "I wrote him and said I'd only give it to him out in the open, in a public place."

Rick nodded, following along. "Then what happened?"

"He told me to bring it to the fight tonight. What's more public than a fight? I waited for him in the lobby of the arena before the fight started. I couldn't get near him when they first came in, Powell was all over him. I decided to wait until the fight started. I wasn't sure where he was sitting, but I knew it would be somewhere near the ring, so I went up top to get a better view.

"I was standing in one of the tunnels, when a man walked by. I recognized him, I'd seen him before, guarding the secretary. He didn't know who I was. There was a woman with him, with red hair. Bright red. I'd never seen her before.

"I knew he was with Kirkland, so I looked to see what he'd do. He and the woman went into the tunnel. They went through a door into a room under the seats—some kind of maintenance area, I guess. I only got a glimpse of it through the open door, I had to be careful, I didn't want them to see me.

"But I saw them. The man was talking to the assassin, the one who killed Kirkland, and—"

"Wait a minute, stop right there," Rick said. "This is Dunne you're talking about? Kevin Dunne? The head of security for the secretary?"

"That's right," Julia said.

"Dunne was talking with Rabat before he shot Kirkland?"

"I recognized him, I'd just seen him come in with Kirkland five minutes before. I didn't know who Rabat was until I saw his picture on TV in the bar."

"You saw wrong. It couldn't be Dunne."

"Just listen to the rest."

Dunne's actions could have been explained as a

security measure. The shaggy-haired man and the red-head could have been undercover agents, part of Secretary Kirkland's protective detail. It would make sense to have a few undercover operatives in civilian dress salted among the crowd for added coverage. Dunne could have been meeting with his agents, briefing or getting briefed by them. Of course the meeting would be clandestine, otherwise the agents wouldn't be undercover anymore.

That must be the reason. So Julia had told herself earlier that night, as she stood in the mouth of Tunnel 26, steeling herself to make contact with the secretary. . . .

She felt ridiculous, she told Rick, in her blonde wig, like a cartoon version of a secret agent, but not so ridiculous that she wanted to take it off and run the risk of being recognized. Whistle-blowing is a hazardous profession.

She spotted the secretary and went down to the arena floor, crossed to him, and sat in Dunne's vacant seat.

After her brief exchange with Rick, Julia put her coat over the seat back, intentionally letting it fall to the floor in front of the secretary. He picked it up and reached to hand it to her.

"It's in the pocket," she said.

It took a moment, but he got it. "You've been writing to me?"

"It's in the envelope."

Kirkland stared at the envelope, which was sticking out of one of the jacket pockets. "What is it?" he asked.

"The satellite infrareds from yesterday's test."

"They already gave me those. They showed convergent impact."

"Now take a look at the real ones," she said. "They gave you doctored copies. These are the originals, from the proving ground computers in White Sands. See for yourself."

The clandestine bug must have been contagious, because now Kirkland was looking around, left and right, to see if anybody was watching. He pulled the envelope from Julia's jacket pocket and lifted the flap.

Inside were a set of what looked like X-ray photos. Kirkland pulled them and began leafing through them, studying them discreetly.

Julia leaned over the back of her chair. "Look at the heat signatures at the moment of impact. The flashes are dots. If the AirGuard made full intercept the way it's supposed to, there would be one dot. But there's two. Every time. The target blows up, but the AirGuard never gets within ten meters of it."

"Then why would the target blow up?" Kirkland asked, genuinely puzzled.

"Because they rigged it, Mr. Secretary. They put on a fireworks display for you."

On the other side of the ring, a drunk stood up, screaming, *"Here comes the pain, baby, here comes the pain!"*

Julia said to Kirkland, "The company knows the system doesn't work, but they're pushing it through anyway."

In the ring, Tyler dropped his guard and Ruiz loosed the uppercut, staggering the champ.

"Up up up, keep your guard up, you idiot!" Rick screamed, rising.

Julia leaned closer to Kirkland so she could be heard over the clamor. "I know what they're thinking—get it approved now, we'll say we're sorry and fix it later," she said.

The crowd roared; she had to shout over it.

"But *you're* the one who's going to be sorry!"

Hearing that, Rick gave her a second glance. But that was all.

"Jesus Christ, Bert Powell is out of his fucking mind," Kirkland said, ashen.

Julia said, "If you deploy that missile system and a war breaks out—"

"I get the picture. Don't make any plans for the next six months, young lady. You're going to be sending some people to jail."

The champ bounced out of the corner, falling flat to the canvas. The crowd jumped up, screaming. Kirkland stood up, too, caught in the grip of the electric moment.

Then the shooting started, and Kirkland was down, shot through the throat.

And Julia, wounded, grabbed the envelope and was running for her life. . . .

Rick and Julia sat on the steps in the stairwell as she finished her story. Rick stared into nowhere, more than a little sick.

"Oh, Christ," he said.

"I'm sorry. I wish I didn't know any of this either," Julia said.

"Then why did you have to stick your nose in where it didn't belong? You were a number cruncher, couldn't you let well enough alone and just crunch the Goddamn numbers?"

"I was doing my job! We're creating a defense system that's supposed to save lives."

Rick rolled his eyes. "Jesus, somebody hands you a line and you just swallow it whole, don't you?"

"I believed in what we're doing, and they've corrupted it. Someone has to speak up; it's important."

She sounded like she believed it and she looked so brave and sincere and yes, *righteous,* that it got Rick really pissed off.

He sneered, "Does it feel important now? Did it feel important when the bullet hit?"

"I have no choice! I don't want innocent soldiers' blood on me."

"Soldiers aren't innocent."

"Whose side are you on, anyway?!"

"My side," Rick said. He rubbed his face, thinking, shaking his head. He'd thought hard to get this far, and now that he'd gotten here, he had to think faster and harder than he ever had in his life, and he didn't have a clue as to how he should jump.

"An E-mail," he said. "Why didn't you just put up a billboard? They saw you coming a mile away, all they had to do was sit back and wait for you to show your face."

"I was careful," Julia said defensively. "I waited till Powell was gone, I didn't sit down until it was clear—"

"Clear? You sat down exactly when they wanted you to. They opened the door and you walked through, right on cue. They didn't miss him with that second shot, they missed *you.*"

"I thought I'd get fired, not killed!"

"When they terminate an employee, they really terminate 'em."

"What do we do now?" Julia asked.

That was the Big Question, but Rick didn't have any answers, not yet.

"Are you a cop, or aren't you?"

Rick knew he should say something, but he was mute, like his lips were glued shut.

"I can't get past the men at the doors by myself, but with you, I'd be fine. Once I'm outside, you can forget all about me. I can take care of myself," Julia said.

"You've done a hell of a job so far."

"Look, I'm sorry if—"

"Oh, please, you're sorry," Rick said in a stone-cold voice.

"What are you mad at me for?!"

"Because I didn't have to know! You decided to have this problem, not me, my world woulda gone right on turning just fine, but now either way I look, I have to do something I don't want to do," Rick said. He recognized the whining tone in his voice as that of every loser who'd ever pleaded with him for a break, and he hated it, but he forced himself to go on.

"You understand what I'm saying? *I do not want to do this!*"

"Do what?" Julia asked. Rick didn't answer. She looked him in the face, trying to read him, but he looked away.

"How old are you?" he asked abruptly.

"Twenty-six."

"Married?"

"No."

"Family around here?"

"My mother, in New York."

"Boyfriend?"

She pulled back, shrinking from him, pressing up against the railing behind her. "Why are you asking me all this?"

"Kevin. Kevin Dunne. You're positive he's the one you saw with Rabat before he fired the shots?"

Julia got it. "Oh, Jesus, you know him."

Did he, really? Rick talked fast. "There were people rushing in front of you, you were nervous and scared— you could be wrong, isn't it possible?"

"Yes," she said definitely, "yes, now that I think about it, I might be mistaken—"

"You're a terrible liar," Rick said, disgusted.

From below came the sound of slamming doors and footsteps pounding on the stairs. Rick grabbed Julia, pulling her to her feet. "Come with me," he said.

She stuffed the manila envelope back under her shirt.

Down they went.

SEVENTEEN

In the conference room, there were two men, Dunne and Powell. Gilbert Powell sat at the head of the table, his customary place. Dunne stood to one side of him, facing him.

Powell looked like what he was, a dynamic corporate boss of the military-industrial variety. "Did you find the girl?" he asked.

"Not yet," Dunne said.

"Not yet," Powell echoed, his voice resonant with power but without emotional shadings, power in reserve, withholding judgement for the moment until all the facts were in.

"But I think the cop I told you about may have," Dunne went on. "With your permission, I'd like to put him in the picture."

"That was never the plan."

"The soft spot in any plan is the human element, sir. People are unpredictable."

"Not this one, you told me," Powell reminded the other, with no heat, simply stating it for the record. Letting Dunne know that it was on the record.

Something rapped against the curtained window behind Powell from outside. Dunne hadn't imagined it—it was a sharp metallic tap-tap-tapping against the windows.

It stopped. Dunne looked at Powell, waiting for his reaction to the tapping. But the tapping didn't come again. Powell held his hands in front of him on the table, fingers pressed together steeple-fashion. He looked up at Dunne intently, studying him with slow, infrequent blinks.

There was a heavy *thunk* outside the window. Dunne glanced that way, unnerved. He unbuttoned his collar button, wiped his forehead.

"It seems our local asset has turned into something of a liability," Powell suggested.

"Not at all. Not at all. Rick has no idea what he's doing. He's like a kid, that's all. He's excited, he's caught up in the moment."

"His psychological state is of no interest to me."

Dunne could feel the moment slipping away from him. "I know Rick, he'll fall in line. Let me at least give him the opportunity."

"Absolutely not. Don't tell him anything, just keep spinning him."

"And if I can't—?"

Thunk.

Dunne flinched, and Powell caught it. "Everything you are, Major—*where* you are—is because *I* put you there," Powell said. "You enjoy the perquisites of money and power. They are not without sacrifice. There is such a thing as the greater good. When mankind builds a bridge, a few men may drown. That does not make the engineers murderers."

Powell pushed back his chair, rising. He went to the curtained windows, standing at one end of them, taking hold of the window cords, and pulling them so the curtains slid back, exposing the windows.

The storm was howling, rattling the windows in their steel frames. Outside, at eye level, the electric beacon globe atop the missile marquee was buffeted by the wind, bobbing wildly. It bumped up against the glass occasionally, going *thunk, thunk.*

Powell's thin smile said, *I'm better than you, that's why I'm in charge.* He turned, faced the windows, and studied the storm. He stood staring with his hands clasped behind his back.

A minute passed before he spoke again.

"Kirkland died ten minutes ago. This is no time for you to get religion. We're locked on a course now, you understand that, don't you, Major?"

"I just—hadn't anticipated some of the specifics, that's all."

"Poor planning is no excuse. What do you think we should have done, Kevin, cancel an entire missile system because of a few bugs? Nobody said it's perfect yet, but it will be perfect, and when it is, it'll save lives. Thousands of lives.

"Kirkland, the great reformer, his hands were as dirty as the rest of them. He was looking for any reason to cancel the system so he could pork barrel the contract to some half-assed company in his own state. He was a crook who got what was coming to him."

It was a long speech for Powell, but he was getting into practice for when he'd make his move into the political arena, and condescend to run for the presidency of the United States, as many friends and admirers were urging him to do.

While Powell was talking, Dunne looked out the window and watched the rain running in sheets across the glass, blurring the candy-colored lights of the gaudy beacon globe.

A wicked gust suddenly blew up, the biggest yet, swelling with awesome violence, seizing the missile marquee and shaking it. The beacon globe smashed into one of the huge, inch-thick windows, pulverizing it.

The window imploded, spewing broken glass into the room, letting in wind and violent rain. The beacon globe swung back into place, bobbing on top of the towering marquee. Some of the pastel lights had broken and were now sputtering, hissing, and sparking in accompaniment with the storm.

Powell had neatly taken a few steps back, avoiding the shards, and was now surveying the damage with wry amusement. Dunne was rattled. Powell put a hand on his shoulder to steady him.

"There is no conscience on a mission, Major, there's only orders. Hesitate for a second and you will find yourself dead."

A veiled threat? Dunne glanced sharply at the older man, but saw only the wise concern of a mentor and leader.

He said, "This is a friend of mine, sir. . . ."

"Fine. Bring him in if you can. I don't like it but I'll

live with it, as a favor to you. But if he shows the slightest reluctance . . ."

Dunne looked at the other, waiting for what he knew was coming.

"Don't piss and moan and talk the job to death, just do it and report back when it's done," Powell said.

"Yes, sir."

"Bringing it all back home," Rick said, pushing open the blue-painted gate of the wooden chute that accessed the people-mover tube construction site.

"I don't understand. What did you say?" Julia asked, like her life depended on it. She was so fucking earnest, thought Rick. Then again, maybe her life did depend on it. On him.

"I was talking to myself," he said. "I was here earlier tonight, that's all. It's a good place."

She looked like she didn't believe him, but she went through the gateway into the chute anyway. He followed her inside, and quickly looked back along the maintenance-level tunnel to see if they were being followed. But there wasn't a soul around.

He closed the gate from the inside and gestured for Julia to go ahead. She followed the chute into the big tube, and he followed her. Before stepping into the tube, he had a crazy thought—what if Cyrus was still there?

Cyrus wasn't there, of course not. Rick hadn't hurt him too badly, just roughed him up a little to teach him a lesson. But Cyrus was able to walk out under his own power, and undoubtedly had, as soon as he could do so.

A handful of powdery white blossoms scattered on the tubeway floor near the chute were the remains of the glass vials Rick had stomped into dust earlier.

The tubeway shook, storm-rocked. Julia looked around, eyes wide. "What *is* this place?" she asked, awed and chilled in equal degrees.

Rick told her. "Gets the suckers into the casino fast, like a big conveyor belt. Or it will be, when it's finished."

He started down the tubeway branch leading down to the Boardwalk, going a few paces before he discovered that Julia wasn't with him, but was hanging behind.

"This way," he said.

She didn't budge. "What does that lead to?"

"The Boardwalk."

"It looks awfully dark down there."

"You don't want a lot of light. Come on, let's go."

She pointed in the opposite direction, at the tubeway branch that sloped upward. "Where does that go?"

"To the casino," Rick said. "Only you can't get in, because it's blocked off. If you want to get in."

"I don't," she said. He started down the tubeway once more, and this time she followed, lingering a few steps behind. The deeper they went into the tube, the closer she got to him, and the darker it got. But there was still enough light shining in through the glass ceiling for them to see by.

The tubeway was shaped like a rocket ship, with the tail opening at the Boardwalk end. There the mouth of the tube belled out, to simulate the spaceship's tail. The bell shape was almost twenty-five feet long from the mouth to the neck, where it narrowed to the same width as the rest of the tube.

At the neck, there was a metal-framed barrier with two doors, one on the right, the other on the left, both opening onto the tube's bell-shaped entryway. A temporary barrier, to be replaced when the construction was done.

Rick turned the knob on the left-hand door, threw it open, and gestured for Julia to enter. When she wouldn't move, he went in first, and she finally followed.

At this end of the tube, the work wasn't quite finished. The archway of the Boardwalk entrance was made of thick concrete blocks, with steel rod framing in the middle of it and thick plywood nailed up outside of it, solidly sealing off access to the sea. It was a dead end, and beyond was the howling storm.

Rick said, "You'll be safe here. I'll be back in half an hour."

"I thought you were getting me out of here!" Julia exclaimed.

"I'm giving you a place to hide. I'll take you out through the hotel when I get back."

"The hotel—!"

Rick started back the way they had come. Julia said, "Wait, where are you going?!"

"I gotta know something for sure."

"Don't leave me alone, you're my only chance to get out of here!"

He stopped and looked back at her. "Boy, did you bet on the wrong horse."

He took off, following the tubeway upward. He passed through agitated patches of light and shadow, his figure dwindling until it was swallowed up by the gloom in the middle of the tubeway.

And Julia was alone. She went to the archway, the tunnel mouth, but the plywood sheeting over the reinforced steel rods was a solid construction job. With a sledgehammer, she might be able to batter her way to a corner of the wooden sheeting, given enough time and strength, for her to slip through it and escape to the outside world.

But there were no tools in the space, nothing she could use as a prybar or battering ram, not even a loose concrete block.

She crossed to the opposite end, to the neck where double doors barred the way. She was surprised to see that both doors were equipped with dead-bolt locks, which fastened from the inside of the entryway.

That was something. She slammed the doors and threw the deadbolts, locking herself in, in this hiding place, which could so easily become an execution cell.

EIGHTEEN

Rick groped around on the floor beside the blue gate inside the chute. He was feeling around for the padlock that he'd taken off this door earlier tonight, when he'd had his little conference with Cyrus. He found the lock pretty much where he remembered leaving it.

On the other side of the fence, the maintenance-level tunnel was empty. Rick eased open the gate and stepped out, shutting it and locking it with the padlock. He didn't want Julia flying the coop in his absence.

He went through the tunnel, onto a stairwell, and up into the arena's above-ground level. He trotted down a corridor, passing the alcove that had been transformed into Lou Logan's makeshift press room. Lou, on an off-camera break between bits, spotted Rick and gave him the high sign. Rick halted, waiting for Lou to dodge around the members of the TV crew who were setting up for another broadcast.

"Hey. Here," Lou said, holding out an envelope stuffed thick with cash. Rick just looked at it, not comprehending.

"It's your five grand. For letting me be the guy," Lou said.

Rick stared numbly as Lou shoved the envelope in his hand and stuffed something else in his shirt pocket.

"You're all heart, Rick," he said.

Rick wouldn't have thought that making five thousand dishonest bucks could taste so flat, but there it was. Lou turned and rejoined the crew, stepping into the bright TV lights.

Rick resumed his journey, walking a couple of dozen yards down the corridor before remembering the envelope in his hand and pocketing it. His mind was a million miles away.

He entered Tunnel 26 and followed it toward the main arena. The passageway and surrounding area was crawling with about a dozen FBI agents, unmistakable in their federal-style suits and ties. They all had the same look, wearing clothing suited to accountants and lawyers— slick accountants and sober corporate lawyers. But most of them were bareheaded. They didn't have to wear hats anymore, as was mandated back in J. Edgar's day. Which was too bad, because on a night like this, hats would have kept the rain off their heads.

They swarmed the crime scene at the tunnel mouth. One of them spotted Rick and put a hand out to stop him.

"Sir, this entire area is now the site of an FBI investigation. I'm afraid you'll have to . . ."

Rick unlimbered his billfold, wearily badging him, and the G-Man let him pass. Rick walked through the tunnel, slowing as he neared the arena end. The lights were bright outside the tunnel mouth. To one side, he saw the double doors of the maintenance area where Julia said she had seen Dunne with Rabat.

He reached the mouth of the tunnel and examined the place from which Rabat had fired. Some of the feds gave him curious looks, but none accosted him. Rabat's body had long since been taken away, with only a chalked body outline marking where he had made his stand. It looked oddly festive, like some kind of stylized graffiti design. The bloodstains weren't so jolly. There were a lot of them. There always are, with head shots.

Rick came out of the tunnel and into the open. He looked back at the tunnel wall behind him, at the big number 26 painted there. Something he remembered having seen earlier in the control booth nagged at him, prickling his mind like a burr.

He looked up at the ceiling of the area. Straight overhead, at the very center, tethered to a stanchion, floated a small blimp fitted with a remote-controlled video camera.

Now he remembered.

He went up to the PPV control booth, where the technicians and the director still labored, wrapping up, closing down. The giant bank of monitors imaged a variety of angles and shots of the nearly empty arena. Two monitors were tuned to local TV stations, one of which was doing a weather report from the Boardwalk, and another which showed Lou Logan popping off on a segment that now was being broadcast live.

"What's the deal with the blimp?" Rick asked.

"It's called a zero-gravity flying eye. New camera, we just got it in this morning," the director said, with the enthusiasm of a hardware nut relishing his latest toy.

"So nobody knew you had it?"

"Well, I knew," the director said, shrugging. "It's remote controlled, we can float it any place we want, for overhead stuff."

"Yeah, I remembered seeing it when I was up here before, but I didn't put it together until now," Rick said. "Let's go to the videotape."

The director hit a few buttons and the image on the screen changed to an aerial view of the arena, looking straight down at the area around Tunnel 26. The tape began crawling in frame-by-frame mode.

Rick went to it, stared at the screen, so close that his breath misted the glass. He had the director play around with the tape until it was set where he wanted it, with Rabat standing in the mouth of the tunnel, pulling something out of the top of his pants leg—a rifle.

Behind him, in the shadows, a figure could be seen standing, waiting. No details, just a figure-shaped outline, a waiting blur.

"I need to look at this part alone," Rick said.

"Okay," the director said, pausing the image. He got up and left, Rick taking his place in the console chair. Rick ran his finger over the play button, not wanting to push it.

But he did.

Time stopped standing still on the monitor as the tape began rolling again. Rabat shook off his inertness and began shucking the rifle out of his pants leg. Shouldering the weapon, he sighted down into the arena, and fired. A spearblade of flame flashed at the tip of the rifle, a muzzle flare, then, after a pause, another.

Behind Rabat, the lurker in the shadows was in

motion, striding forward, holding a gun at the end of an outstretched arm. Dunne.

A pause, then a spear of fire leaped from the bore of Dunne's weapon, fired at the back of Rabat's skull at point-blank range. Brains and bone erupted, bloody mists enhaloing Rabat's head. Rabat fell forward, face-first.

"What the fuck is the matter with these people?" asked a voice from behind Rick.

Dunne's.

It was disorienting, seeing Dunne's image on screen, and hearing him speaking in person in the control booth. Rick turned and saw the real Dunne, whoever that was, standing in the doorway to the trailer.

"They were specifically told they couldn't mount a camera on the ceiling," he said.

Everybody was staring at him, the director and the technicians, Rick. Dunne told the others, "Out."

The technicians filed out the door without a word. The director started to object, but Dunne cut him off sharply, asking, "You like working for Powell Pay-Per-View Television?"

Actually, the director loathed it, but he hated the idea of the unemployment line even worse. He started to gather up some of his things, but Dunne said, "You can get them later. Get out."

The director exited, leaving Dunne alone in the booth with Rick. Dunne looked around, shaking his head.

"Eighteen angles is enough now? They gotta have an eye in the sky, they want to see what God sees?" He noticed Rick staring. "Don't give me that wounded look. You don't have the face for it," he said.

He noticed something on one of the monitors. "Oh,

hey. Watch this," he said, leaning over and turning up the sound.

On the screen, Gilbert Powell, bloodstained and bedraggled, stepped heavily up to the microphone in Lou Logan's statement room, blinking from the harsh glare of the TV lights. Blinking back tears.

He said, his voice unsteady, his face lined with suffering and compassion, "I've just received word from the Atlantic City Medical Center—Secretary Charles Evans Kirkland is dead.

"He passed away at 10:47 P.M. I want to extend my deepest sympathies to the secretary's family, and to the people and the government he so faithfully served— even to offering up the supreme sacrifice on behalf of the country he loved so well."

He paused, wiped away a tear, then forged on, his voice gathering strength. "And . . . and I have something else to say. To those who would try to bully us, to terrorize us, to divert us from the causes of peace and democracy, I say—"

Dunne turned off the sound and looked at Rick. "The Man's got it all together. That's what's called the first draft of history. And it's going to hold, Rick."

"I was so proud of you. You were the one who was different. You made it out of here."

"You can take the boy out of Atlantic City . . ."

"You got out of the shit, you were doing a big job, serving the country—"

"Rah rah. Don't you wave the flag at me," Dunne said. "Where is she?"

Rick's gaze lost some of its wounded quality, and he looked up at Dunne with gunsight eyes. "You were the missing fifth."

160

"What?"

"The fifth. Remember, Kevin? The shooter, the red-head, the drunk, Tyler, and the fifth plotter, the one who was on the other end of the radio, giving the go signal—you, Kevin."

"People are unpredictable," Dunne said, shaking his head. "Who'd have figured that you'd get so smart? . . . And what a time to do it in." His voice held grudging admiration.

"Look at me and tell me I'm wrong, Kevin."

That's not what Dunne told him.

The whistle-blower's identity was unknown. That was the key variable in the equation. They'd been monitoring Secretary Kirkland's E-mail, monitoring all his communications, in fact, so they knew there was an informant somewhere out there, or rather in there, in the Powell organization, but they didn't know who it was. When Kirkland arranged a meeting with the unknown source, to be held at the heavyweight championship fight in Atlantic City, the plotters knew the crisis had arrived.

The mysterious source was the soft spot in the plan, requiring the flexibility to improvise and adapt on the spot with a variety of contingency plans, right up to and including the final seconds of zero hour.

If the whistle-blower could be identified before linking up with Kirkland, well and good. That was the best-case scenario. But if the informant did succeed in making contact, the plotters would have to go to Plan B: neutralizing Kirkland. And of course, the informant.

The components of the assassination machine were easily assembled. Rabat was a certified mental case with known links to Middle East terrorist groups. Plus he could shoot, unlike, say, Lee Harvey Oswald, thus disposing of the need for a backup shooter. Rabat was shooter and patsy both, all wrapped up in one nice neat package.

To assassinate someone important, the best way is to work through the bodyguards. History is full of examples, such as when the Praetorian Guards turned against their emperor, slew him, and put a new Caesar on the throne. That was where Dunne came in. As head of the Department of Defense's protective detail covering the secretary, he was the pivot man for the plot. His two main subordinates on the detail were his creatures, ambitious underlings who could be relied on to do what had to be done.

Tyler and Ruiz were easy to get to. They were owned and operated by the big fight syndicates, and would do what they were told. And they weren't told much—only that Tyler was going to take a dive in the first round. They knew nothing about the real purpose of the setup. They figured it was just one more scam for the insiders to make a killing betting on the outcome of the fight.

Zeitz and Serena were pros, in it for the money, with no illusions.

The setup was a sucker trap, designed to flush out the informant. The secretary and Powell were in place in their second-row ringside seats. Those particular seats had been carefully selected in advance, to put Kirkland in the optimum sitting-duck position.

When the opening bell of the fight sounded, the plot began to unfold. Dunne got out of his seat and "confronted" Serena, opening up a sight line between the shooter and the secretary, thanks to the now-vacant front-row seat.

Serena got up and left, Dunne following. They went up the stairs into Tunnel 26. That's where Julia had coincidentally spotted Dunne, on her way into the arena. She knew who Dunne was, having seen him before, honchoing the secretary's security squad. But she didn't know that he was a conspirator.

He didn't know who she was either, had no idea that the blonde in the white pantsuit was the mystery informant whose efforts to alert Kirkland to the truth about the AirGuard had set the assassination plot into motion. If he had known, he could have neutralized her then and there, and the secretary would have lived, never knowing how closely he'd been brushed by the wings of the Death Angel.

But he didn't know, and so . . .

Dunne and Serena went through the door in the tunnel that accessed the maintenance area under the bleachers. The room served as a combination staging area and observation post. Rabat was already inside waiting, according to plan. He hadn't had to smuggle the rifle into the building; it had been smuggled into the maintenance room earlier.

Rabat was the real deal, an extremist eager to strike a blow against what he thought of as the Zionist imperialists and their running-dog lackeys in the Great Satan of the government of the United States.

Julia had caught a glimpse of Dunne huddling with Rabat under the bleachers, but shrugged it off as some routine security tradecraft ploy. She went to the tunnel mouth, looking down at ringside for Kirkland.

Under the bleachers, there were horizontal slits set in the wall at eye level, giving a clear sight line into the

163

arena. An observation post. Dunne took up a position there, with a pair of binoculars and a radio handset.

Julia went down the stairs to the arena floor. From his vantage point, Dunne peered down at the secretary's row through binoculars.

Rabat stuffed the rifle down the right leg of his baggy pants and stiff-legged it out to the tunnel mouth, waiting for the ring action that would be his cue to kill.

Dunne almost gave it the go when he saw the late-comer moving down the aisle, closing in on the secretary. The whistle-blower making contact? No, just a citizen who was looking for his seat in the wrong place, and who moved on when he discovered his mistake.

The blonde in the white suit came down the aisle a minute later, sitting down in the empty seat in front of the secretary.

"Possible make," Dunne said into the radio. Through the binoculars, he saw the secretary pull a large manila envelope from the pocket of Julia's jacket.

"Make is good. Stand by," Dunne radioed.

In the ring, Tyler popped a good hard one into Ruiz's head, dropping him to his knees. The challenger got back up.

Dunne watched Kirkland studying the photos from the envelope. He spoke into the handset. "Start the car."

At ringside, Zeitz heard the message in his earpiece and replied, speaking into a microtransmitter which was disguised as a button on his cuff. "Copy," he said.

No stopping now, the machinery was in motion. Dunne gave the radio to Serena for her to dispose of later. He checked his gun and stepped into the tunnel, holding it under his coat. He stood a half-dozen paces or so behind Rabat, who was unaware of him.

At ringside, Zeitz stood up and screamed at Tyler: *"Here comes the pain, baby, here comes the pain!"*

Ruiz loosed his phantom punch, and the champ went into his act, stumbling backward into a corner. Ruiz charged, windmilling a flurry of rights and lefts.

Tyler flopped out of the corner and hit the canvas. The crowd went nuts, leaping to its collective feet, shrieking.

Kirkland stood up, too, giving Rabat a clear sight line to his target. He squeezed the trigger once, hitting Kirkland, then again, grazing Julia as she was shoved out of the way by Rick.

Dunne stepped up behind Rabat and shot him in the back of the head.

Case closed.

NINETEEN

Case closed?

"Well, not quite," Dunne said, after he had finished telling Rick the way the deal really went down. He didn't like to brag, but Rick thought he was so Goddamned smart, it was a pleasure to show him how he'd been worked by the plotters, spun not once but continuously.

Rick sat there in front of the monitor, gazing blankly at the frozen image of Dunne delivering the *coup de grace* to the assassin, Rabat.

"All that's left now is to tie up the loose ends," Dunne said. "Where is she?"

Rick looked at the other. "Why'd you want me next to you? Why'd it have to be me?"

"What're friends for? I had ninety minutes to cover, and a lot to get done. I needed a cop in charge who was smart enough to look the other way if he saw too much."

"You used me."

That was so self-evident that Dunne didn't even bother to reply. "No offense, Ricky, but I didn't count on you getting as far as you did. That unpredictable human factor again. Your instincts for keeping your head down used to be better than this.

"Let's get this over with. Where is she?"

"She didn't do nothing wrong. She was just trying to save some guys' lives. Soldiers. You know, like you used to be."

"I'm not going to argue ideology with a guy who finds an envelope full of cash in his squad car every Friday. What is it you want, Rick? Come on, you're good with numbers. Three hundred grand? Four hundred? You hit a fifty to one shot here, all you have to do is cash in the ticket."

"This the clean money you were talking about before?" Shaken, Rick fumbled in his shirt pocket and pulled out his pack of cigarettes. As he pulled them out, something else fell out along with them, fluttering to the floor, whatever it was that Lou Logan had shoved in there earlier.

Dunne asked, "Don't you think Angela would like a few nice things for once in her life? Don't you think she deserves them?"

Not listening, Rick bent down and picked up whatever had fallen from his pocket. It was a bloodstained hundred dollar bill, the bloody Ben he had taken from Cyrus and later passed back and forth with Lou.

"Jinx money. It figures," Rick said dully, hollow-eyed.

Dunne frowned, not getting it, too busy selling. "All I'm asking for is the location of one person at one moment in time."

Rick looked at Dunne and mumbled something inaudible.

"What?" Dunne asked.

"I said, I never killed nobody."

"Stop it," Dunne said scornfully. "Who said anything about killing anyone?"

"That's a good one."

"We just want to talk to her, find out what she wants. Maybe she has a little more common sense than you. Look, she isn't your problem, let her be mine. Just name one little hiding place in this great big hotel, and I guarantee you'll never hear a word about any of this again."

Rick had nothing to say.

Dunne went on, "What's the alternative, pal? You think you're gonna make a heroic stand, expose the whole thing? Wise up. You're the wrong guy to play shining knight. You'll be alone in a spotlight, and guys like you can't stand up to that light. You'll burn up under it. They start looking for dirt on you, it'll be a mudslide. Forget about your job, start thinking about jail. You know how they love cops in jail, Ricky."

Dunne leaned over the monitor that held the incriminating tape. He reached for the VCR under it, the one that held the master tape from that camera angle. He hit a button and the tape began to rewind, zipping the blurred images backward to the fight.

Dunne said, "Your girlfriend'll be gone at the first sign of trouble, but not before she has a little chat with Angela, so say good-bye to your wife, too. You like that house in Margate, don't you? Gone. The kids? Twice a month ain't so bad, if you can get 'em to spend the night in your shitty apartment.

"You will lose it *all,* my friend, everything in your whole connected life will fall the fuck apart. And you'll take me down in the process."

He hit another button on the VCR and the screen went blue. The word "Erase" appeared in the lower right-hand corner.

Rick reached to stop the tape, and Dunne started to pull his gun. Rick froze when the weapon cleared the holster. Meanwhile, the tape kept erasing.

"Kevin. Wow, man. They tell you to take me out?"

Dunne was shaking as he put the gun back in its holster. "I'm under a lot of fucking pressure here, all right? Why can't you just do like you always do?

"*Please* be smart. You're all alone on this."

Rick shook his head. "No. You forgot Tyler. If he talked to me, he'll talk to somebody else."

Dunne crossed to the control-booth door, and opened it. He leaned out the doorway, motioning to somebody outside. He leaned back inside, making way for Lincoln Tyler to enter the booth.

"Lincoln and I have come to an understanding," Dunne said.

Behind Tyler stood two security agents, Dunne's sidemen.

"It's shaping up like old home week in here," Rick said.

Tyler shifted uncomfortably, looking as if he wanted to be somewhere, anywhere else. The security duo looked at Rick like he was already dead and buried.

"You got nothin', kiddo, you crapped out," Dunne said. "Snake eyes. The house wins. . . . Where is she?"

Rick was silent. Dunne looked at his watch, seeing the seconds tick past. When it was obvious that Rick wouldn't talk, Dunne turned to the agents. "Okay, grab him," he said.

The duo braced Rick, hauling him up out of his chair and taking his weapon.

"A lifetime of looking out for Number One, and you have to turn idealistic now, of all times," Dunne marveled. "Talk about self-destructive! You must want it all to come crashing down on you."

"It's like the old movie about two guys growing up in the same neighborhood, and one guy turns out to be the judge who sends the other guy to the chair," Rick said. "Only this time, it's the judge who's the real killer."

"That's the difference between real life and the movies, pal. Case closed," Dunne said.

He turned to the others. "Let's go, it's getting latc."

TWENTY

They hustled Rick out of the control booth, through a service door, into a stairwell, and down into the lower levels of the building, through a maze of tunnels and into the loading dock with the sliding metal overhead bay doors. Sheets of rain pounded into the doors from outside, ringing hollowly through the cavernous space of the garage.

Dunne led the way, followed by Rick flanked by the two agents, each holding one of his arms above the elbow to prevent him from making a break. Tyler followed, walking a few paces behind the others.

Dunne halted, the others following suit. The agents let go of Rick's arms and stepped away from him, but not too far, keeping close to him so they'd be there if he started acting up.

"One last time," Dunne said. "Where is she, Rick? *Where is she, Goddamn it?!*"

Rick looked him in the face and smiled with only his lips. Dunne twitched, impatient.

"Okay, fun time is over," he said. "What do you say we have a little boxing match of our own?"

He nodded to Tyler, who stepped forward reluctantly, raising his fists. They were big fists, huge, like the rest of him.

"Aw, come on," Rick said.

"Jesus, what are the odds on this one, about five million to one?" Dunne said.

Tyler spoke, breaking a silence that he had held since he'd first entered the control booth. In a dull monotone, he said to Rick, "Just tell him what he wants to know."

"Think you're gonna get out of this alive? They'll bury you, too," Rick said.

"Not me," Tyler said, shaking his head. "I'm a money-spinner. Dead, I can't headline those fights, bring in those big money gates."

"After tonight, your next fight will be at Wrestlemania."

"That hurt. I remember you from high school now. You were a dickhead then, and you're a dickhead now."

Rick turned to Dunne, trying to make him see reason. "Kevin, I can't, man. This is over the line for me. Everybody's got a line, somewhere. Don't make me do it. Please."

Dunne gave Tyler the nod. "Round one."

Tyler moved in, looming, inexorable. Rick figured his one-in-a-million chance was to disable Tyler at the start, with some dirty fighting.

He faked with his hands, trying to distract Tyler while launching a vicious kick at his knee. If it had connected, it would have busted his kneecap, crippling him.

It never came close. Tyler easily sidestepped, brushing aside Rick's guard and slamming a quick one-two to his ribs. His fists hit like cannonballs. Rick crumpled, groaning.

Dunne winced. "Sounded like a couple of broken ribs to me. Can we stop now? Where is she?"

Rick struggled to his feet and gamely put up his guard. Dunne nodded to Tyler and turned away, looking down. Water was leaking into the garage from under the overhead doors, and Dunne was standing in a deepening puddle.

Tyler's fists flashed—a soft right to the kidneys, a left to the gut, and a short hard chop to the side of Rick's face.

Rick fell again. He lay on his side, hugging himself.

Tyler said, "At least *try,* man."

"I am trying," Rick said, having trouble forming the words with his smashed mouth. Drooling blood, he pawed the air, groping for a hanging cable and grabbing it, using it to pull himself back up on his feet. He hauled himself up agonizingly hand by hand, like climbing a rope in gym class. He would have fallen, if not for the cable.

He launched himself at Tyler, hoping to catch him unaware with a roundhouse right. But Tyler's head wasn't there, and the fist connected with empty air.

Tyler counted with a few quick jabs, peppering Rick's face. Rick staggered but stayed up, weaving. His lips were smashed, blood pouring from his mouth.

Dunne moved in close to him. "You'll go through all this and you won't change a thing, Rick. Guys like you don't have that effect on the world.

"For the last time—*where is she?!*"

Rick hawked up a big bloody gob and spat it on the front of Dunne's uniform, spraying it across the medals and ribbons pinned to his breast.

That did it for Dunne. "Put him out," he said.

Rick couldn't even raise his fists, it was all he could do just to stay on his feet. Tyler stepped in, and said, "Watch the birdie."

He popped one to Rick's chin. Lightning flashed inside Rick's skull as his head snapped back and his legs went out from under him.

The next thing he knew, he had a worm's-eye view of the floor, where he lay sprawling. He didn't remember going down. A pair of shoes moved into his field of vision, slim narrow shoes ruined by water stains and streaks.

Their owner hunkered down, crouching beside Rick, and now he could see it was Dunne. Dunne put one hand on Rick and spoke to him softly.

"If it were anybody but me, you'd be dead," Dunne said. He rose, straightening up, and gestured to the others to move out. They headed for the door.

"Stay outside the door," Dunne told one of the agents. "I'll be back in half an hour."

They went out, leaving Rick alone.

There wasn't much of Rick left, and what there was, was hurting. That's what was left, the hurt and the darkness. He welcomed the hurt because it held back the darkness, keeping him conscious.

He rolled on his side, struggling to his hands and knees.

He lay flat on the floor, face down. He must have blacked out. He tried again, and this time when he got to

176

his hands and knees, he stayed. He thought he was going to throw up or pass out, but he did neither.

He felt like he had been worked over with baseball bats. He wondered if he was busted up inside. His ribs were sore, aching, maybe cracked, but they didn't feel broken. That was something. His face felt funny, like something had been knocked off-kilter. One eye was swollen almost shut, all he could see out of it was a slit, but the other eye was okay. His smashed mouth and chin were numb, but when he pressed the back of his hand there, it came away wet and sticky with blood.

He hurt all over, except for his hands, the one part of him that hadn't come into contact with Tyler.

He couldn't crouch here hugging himself forever, but he knew that if he tried to stand up by himself, he'd fall down. He crawled on hands and knees to the workbench, using it for handholds as he hauled himself to a standing position. Then he held onto the bench to keep from falling down.

He stood hunched forward like a little old man. He let go of the workbench and didn't fall over, but somehow managing to stay on his feet. He started forward, taking little, shuffling steps.

The exit door seemed a mile away. He pointed himself toward it and started shuffling, moving his feet like a cross-country skier. It felt like he was struggling against waist-high snowdrifts. How pleasant it would be to drop off into them, those white billows, drowning in the painless dark. . . .

How much time did he have? "I'll be back in half an hour," Dunne had said, but Rick didn't know how long he'd been passed out on the floor. Too long.

But he was up and moving, and getting stronger. There

was still something of him left, and he was able to draw on it and keep going.

When he reached the door, he was ready for a wheelchair, but that wasn't in the cards. What he needed was a weapon. A weapon, and a new body. On a wheeled cart he found a piece of pipe, twelve inches long, and heavy. It had a nice heft in his hand. Too bad it wasn't a crutch.

The exit door wasn't locked. He opened it a crack, pressed his good eye to it, and looked out into the corridor. To the left, about a dozen paces away, stood one of the security agents, his back turned to Rick. He stood leaning against the wall, looking the other way.

Rick's hand tightened on the metal pipe. He would have jumped the guy for sure if he'd thought he could manage to cross the distance between them without fainting.

To the right, the corridor extended a couple of feet, before opening on a crossway. The short passage was empty.

Stealth was a possibility, one of the few left available to him. If he only had a gun. . . . But he didn't, so he put sneakiness to work. He eased open the door wide enough for him to pass through it, trying not to make any noise. Motors and pumps worked in the area, their muffled chugging masking any slight sounds he might have made.

If the agent should happen to turn around, or even glance back over his shoulder at the door . . .

But he didn't. Rick eased out into the corridor, and shut the door to the loading dock so that everything would look like it was going according to plan, Dunne's plan. Rick had a few plans of his own, if he should somehow manage to get out of this alive.

With one hand against the wall, he crept down the short passage and around the corner, getting away without being detected by the guard.

He was still in the game after all. He lurched forward, putting a few twists and turns and straightaways between him and the garage. Every now and then, a flat glob of blood would spill from his mouth, spattering on the concrete pathways.

At least this area wasn't too far from the service tunnel leading to the entryway to the tube; they were both on the same sublevel of the building.

Rick threaded the corridors as fast as he could force himself to move. Cold sweat poured out of him with every step, but once he got some momentum going, he was able to stagger along at a fair pace.

He kept looking back over his shoulder to make sure he wasn't being followed. To his surprise, he wasn't, but he kept a tight grip on the piece of pipe, a caveman with a club.

He hobbled out of a corridor into the service tunnel, a blue barrier at its far end. He stumbled forward, trying to go too fast, and a searing pain in his guts forced him to one knee. A loud clang sounded as the pipe fell from his nerveless hand, ringing on the floor. It sounded like a timekeeper's bell, signaling the next round.

Time to come out of his corner, scrapping. Or maybe he'd just die here of internal bleeding instead. He thought not. He forced himself up and limped closer toward the blue barrier.

A couple of dozen yards later, he noticed that his hand was empty and remembered he'd neglected to pick up the pipe after dropping it. Too late to go back for it now. It was all he could do to keep moving forward.

The director and a couple of technicians were back in the PPV control booth, getting ready to wrap it up and close it down. A bank of monitors showed the worsening storm outside from various angles. One screen showed a playful gust of wind picking up a jitney and throwing it like a football down the Boardwalk.

"This is great stuff!" the director said. "We could sell it to local. Who can we put out there for a stand-up?"

He turned around and saw Anthea, freshly returned from her recent outdoor stint. She stood just inside the doorway of the booth, soaking wet, taking off her dripping raincoat.

The director had a big broad grin. "Hey, Anthea!"

"Don't even think it, you dog," she said. But she went.

Rick stood outside the blue fence, struggling with the padlocked gate. He leaned against the gate to keep from falling over while he dug in his jeans pockets for the key ring. He fished the keys out and held them up to the light, what light there was, squinting at them with his good idea, trying to guess which key had done the trick. He remembered that he had tried three keys of similar shape before unlocking it earlier, so he fingered through the ring key by key, until he found the three he was looking for.

The second key did the trick. He opened the lock, took it off the hasp, and shouldered the gate open, staggering into the short chuted walkway, reeling. He shut the gate behind him, then threw away the lock, tossing it aside.

Too late he realized that it could have served as a weapon, like brass knuckles, something to fill his hand with. Hit somebody with one of those and you'd lay him out pretty good.

Too late now. Too bad he'd left his keys in it, too. Oh well, fuck 'em.

He went through the chuteway, into the people-mover tube. The storm raged wilder than ever, but inside the tube it was still bone-dry. The builders had done a helluva job.

Too bad they made it so damned long. The Boardwalk branch of the tube tilted down and down and down. Rick set his steps on the path and started his final descent.

Rain sheeting over the top of the tunnel made a rushing sound like an underground river. Rick couldn't hear his own footsteps. The air was thick, steamy. The path sloped downward, through seething masses of shadow and light.

Nearing the dimness at the bottom of the tubeway, he could make out the darker shape of the barrier beyond it, the double doors enclosing the entryway of the tube's belled mouth.

Down there a crash sounded, making Rick jump. The walls of the tube vibrated. The blow, whatever it was, was not repeated. Rick drew closer to the doors.

On the other side of them, Julia crouched in the murkiness of the cell she had locked herself into. She huddled near the doors, to one side of them, back against the wall. The tremendous crash that had just struck was caused by a chunk of flying debris, which smashed into the plywood sheeting over the entrance, splintering open a seam between two sheets, letting in some of the wind and the rain. The split was only a few inches wide, nothing she could exploit as a possible escape route.

Wind screamed through it, like a teakettle on the boil,

venting its steam whistle. The shrilling got on Julia's nerves, which were already strained to the breaking point. She sat as far away from it as she could, hands covering her ears.

The storm that the local powers had gambled would veer out to sea was instead coming ashore. Hurricane Jezebel was here.

Now, the surf pounded the Boardwalk, slamming it with destructive glee, the beach totally submerged. A large wave crashed against the barrier, jetting mountains of spray. A section of guardrail as long as a football field was ripped away like so much tinsel. Wooden planks were torn from the Boardwalk and tossed to the winds like straw.

In front of the arena, the marquee tower swayed, bobbing like a bedspring. A blast of wind sent it slamming into the building, demolishing the windows of the conference room.

The impact tore the globe beacon ball free of the tower. Cables snapped, live wires spit showers of sparks. The globe went dark. It slid down the front of the building and bounced down the stairs, into the courtyard, a loose juggernaut.

The courtyard was hip-deep in seawater, which had been flung there by the waves that were now rolling across the Boardwalk. The globe ebbed back and forth, rising when the waves broke, lowering as much of the water was sucked back by the furious undertow. But the next wave would advance even farther, thrusting land-ward.

The waves set the globe rolling, first this way, then

182

that. It made a low rumbling, grinding sound, like a giant steamroller.

Debris flew past, almost horizontal in the stiff winds. A lamppost leaned, bent, and tore loose at the base, like a tree torn up by its roots. It fell, going dark. The waves had a new toy to play with, and they twisted the steel post like a length of ribbon.

The water had pooled in front of the arena, where there were stone walls and risers and pavilions to hold it in, but farther north along the Boardwalk, the water was only about ankle-deep. That didn't make it any more pleasant for Anthea and the cameraman who had gone outside to satisfy the director's demand for more good storm footage.

A video van was parked on the Boardwalk, fronting the fenced-in grounds of the Millennium construction site, not far from the boarded-up tubeway mouth. The van was anchored down with chock blocks wedged under the tires, as further protection against being swept away. Rain pelted its sheet-metal roof like a Texas hailstorm.

Anthea and the cameraman huddled in the lee of the van, which slightly blunted the storm's force. Anthea clung to a handgrip, her clothes billowing around her in the ferocious wind.

She said—*shouted*—"I'd sure like to know what the fuck I did wrong to get all the shit assignments!"

"Just roll so we can get out of here," the cameraman pleaded. He crouched with the portapak video camera squatting on his shoulder like some futuristic piece of weaponry.

"Holy shit, the van's rocking!" Anthea said, worried. "C'mon!"

She counted on her fingers, "In five four three two one . . ." She was on, and went into her bit. "Well, it seems Tropical Storm Jezebel may just be a hurricane after all. . . ." she began.

It was a long, hard fight, but he made it. Rick was just ten feet away from the two doors at the end of the tunnel, when someone called his name.

"Rick," Dunne said.

Rick froze, then turned around, slowly, painfully. Dunne stood about ten feet away, holding a gun in one hand and the portable locator module in the other.

It was all too sickeningly clear to Rick that he'd been played once again. He reached behind him, feeling around where Dunne had put a hand on his back when he'd given him the kiss-off in the loading dock. His fingers encountered a hard metal burr stuck to the back collar of his jacket. He tore it off, plucking it like it was a particularly noxious insect.

Rick held it pinched between his thumb and forefinger, held it up to the light. It was one of those roach-clip things, the metal alligator clip with the microtracking bulb at one end.

Rick angrily threw it away, wiping his fingers on his pants like it was something unclean.

"That's okay, it's served its purpose," Dunne said. "So has this." He put the locator module in his pocket. The gun stayed out, leveled at Rick's middle.

"Sometimes people are predictable," Dunne said. "Thanks for not letting me down. You did just exactly what I hoped you'd do, what I figured you'd do. That's why I told Tyler to bust you up a little, not too much, but enough to make it convincing and still leave you able to walk around, so you could lead me to the girl."

"My pal," Rick said.

"I tagged you with that little tracking bug, wound you up, and told my men to let you run loose, let you do what comes naturally. I didn't have to worry about losing you, not with the locator bird-dogging you. You picked a pip of a hiding place, I'll give you that. I never would have found it by myself.

"So here we are," Dunne said.

"Where's that?"

"You took the long odds, Rick. That's not like you. Tell her to open the door. You have my word—you will walk away from this. The same deal still goes. It's just her. Not you.

Dunne paused, then said, "Well?"

"I'm thinking," Rick replied.

"That's where you went wrong in the first place."

TWENTY-ONE

The ball globe rocked and shuddered on the Boardwalk like some medieval war machine that had gotten away from its handlers. A wave lifted and sent it rolling north, away from the arena. The wind gave it another boost in the same direction.

It could be heard crunching and grinding, even over the storm. The cameraman held onto the side of the video van with one hand while pointing the camera at it.

The director was loving the footage of the ball bouncing over the planks, splintering them, slamming up against walls and rebounding to roll around some more.

"Great stuff!" he said into the handset. "You look great, Anthea! Can you get any closer to that globe?"

"No!"

The rumbling penetrated into the tunnel, more felt than heard, like a subway train a couple of blocks away coming fast. Dunne was starting to lose it.

He stomped around, waving the gun. "You hear that mother out there?! You think I've got anything left to lose?! Tell her to open the door!"

Rick had lost control of the play—or had he ever really been *in* control of it? He needed to take the play away from Dunne, but how? Was there anything he could use for an edge, leverage?

He and Julia had used the left-hand door of the entryway. Maybe there was something in that. . . .

Dunne was close to the edge. Rick held up a hand in a placating gesture. He veered off to the door on the right, hoping like hell that Julia was not behind it.

Dunne crowded in closer, no more than a few feet away, but not close enough for a sudden lunge to do Rick any good. Rick pounded on the right-hand door. "It's me! Open up!" he said, shouting loud to be heard over the storm.

Dunne waved him aside with the gun. Rick stepped back, standing in front of the door on the left. Dunne's weapon was pointed at the other door.

On the other side of the doors, Julia heard him and reached for the dead bolt. She unlocked it, gripping the doorknob.

She heard a roaring sound from outside and paused, hand on the doorknob.

A burly wave shouldered on to the Boardwalk, rushing, crashing, foaming, and fizzing. The water reached its farthest advance yet, rushing through the open seams of the plywood sheeting at the tunnel mouth, surging inside before it receded.

The sucking undertow sent the globe skittering along

the wall of the Millennium's fenced-in construction site, like a rubber ball being swept along in a rainy gutter.

A panel truck with Dunne's two agents inside it bulled its way up to the outside of the tunnel mouth. Earlier, when Dunne had learned from the locator that Rick was in the tubeway, he had ordered them to proceed to the Boardwalk entrance. That way, the quarry would be bottled up in the tube at both ends, with no chance of escape. That was another ace up Dunne's sleeve, one that Rick didn't even know about.

Keeping the rendezvous with their chief wasn't easy. It had taken a long time and a lot of sweat to muscle the panel truck down the relatively short distance from the outside of the loading docks to the Boardwalk. They had to pass over open muddy ground, and almost got stuck a couple of times.

The truck was in position now, squatting near the tunnel mouth. The agents squatted in the cab, feeling the truck shake. Their instructions were to stay put at the RZ point until Dunne radioed them further instructions. Until then, they were forbidden to break radio silence, so that a suddenly squawking radio wouldn't go off in Dunne's pocket and risk alerting his prey.

The agents were good at following orders, so there they sat, worrying at each new advance of the waves. They were still on high ground, so far. The motor was running, but it couldn't be heard more than a few feet away, thanks to the storm. So Dunne, Rick, and Julia didn't know it was there.

Anthea and the cameraman saw it. "What are those idiots playing at?!" asked the cameraman.

She said, "We're the idiots for staying out here!"

Alarmed by the growing chaos outside, Julia turned back to the door and started to turn the knob.

"Julia?! It's Rick, come on, open the door right now!" He saw the doorknob of the left-hand door turning and quickly looked away, praying that Dunne hadn't seen it.

But Dunne was concentrating on the right-hand door. He raised his gun to about chest height and started squeezing the trigger, pumping slugs through the door, emptying most of the clip in a target cluster no larger than a man's palm.

Julia screamed as the shots ripped through the door next to hers. They stitched through a plywood section at the tunnel mouth, punching big holes through it.

The wood flapped open a few inches, and then the winds counterpunched, grabbing hold of an eight-by-eight plywood square and ripping it off the tunnel mouth with a shrill screeching sound.

With the barrier breached, the tunnel mouth was exposed to the full fury of the storm.

Dunne stood in front of the door, jaws working, eyes glinting, his focus narrowed to the bullet holes smoking in the wood panel. That's when Rick made his move, lunging, barreling into Dunne. He got a grip on the wrist of Dunne's gun hand, pushing it away from him as he shouldered Dunne into the tunnel wall.

Dunne was knocked off-balance, his limbs tangled up with Rick's. Rick kneed him between the legs, hard. Dunne started to fold up. Rick hit him with a forearm elbow smash that sent Dunne's head whipping around in the opposite direction. Rick followed through with another vicious elbow strike, planting it in Dunne's ear. Dunne's head hit the wall, his eyes fogging.

Rick crowded him, working the knee, but Dunne blocked it with his thigh. Rick got a forearm against Dunne's neck, trying to crush his larynx with it. Dunne ducked his head, using his chin to block the strangulation ploy.

All the time, Rick held Dunne's gun hand, slamming it into the wall, trying to get him to drop the gun. But Dunne wouldn't let go. Neither would Rick.

In the panel truck, the two agents had heard the shots, but they figured that it was just Dunne tieing up loose ends, so they decided to stay put.

Then they saw something rising from the sea, something massive, and they knew that they'd made the mistake of their lives.

A wall of water rose above the Boardwalk, thrusting up, climbing, curling, reaching landward.

The Big One was here, the megawave, the crusher. It slouched toward the shore and leaned too far forward, toppling, bringing down hundreds, thousands of tons of seawater.

Julia, crouching beside door, peered out and saw Rick wrestling with Dunne, locked in savage hand-to-hand combat. Without thinking, she ran out the door, into the tunnel.

Dunne landed a short hard jab to Rick's ribs, where Tyler had pummeled him. Rick turned white-hot, then icy cold. That was the finisher.

Dunne shook free and staggered toward the doors, still holding the gun. He skittered, his slick-soled shoes slipping on the wet wooden walkway. He fell to one knee, resting a hand on the ground.

Rick got his feet under him and pushed himself against the wall, trying to rise. He hugged himself, his face leaden, blood spilling from a corner of his mouth.

Julia stood behind him, trying to help him up. Somehow he managed to rise.

Dunne was on his feet, facing them, his back to the doors, the left-hand door flung open. His tussle with Rick had left him feeling none too chipper. His face was red and swollen, bruised where Rick had elbowed it. He had a nosebleed and a split lip and major aches and pains, but he also had a gun.

Rick moved in front of Julia, holding her behind him.

Dunne said, "Get out of the way, Rick!"

"I'm not moving."

"Get out of the way or I'll shoot right the fuck through you!"

"No, you won't."

"Won't I?!"

"Everybody's got a line, Kevin. Don't they?"

Dunne held the gun at arm's length, extended in front of him, pointed at Rick's heart.

And now they all heard the roaring of the coming wave.

The agents in the panel truck decided to disobey orders and get the hell out of there, but too late. The engine gunned but the wheels lost their traction on a surface that was a sheet of rushing seawater. They skittered a hundred feet south of the tunnel before the wave hit them broadside, toppling the truck on its aside. The ocean rushed into the cab.

Anthea and the cameraman cowered inside the video

van, hoping it was on high ground enough to escape the wave.

The wave picked up the globe, skimming it along like a beach ball, tossing it at the tunnel entrance.

Dunne still had the gun pointed at Rick. "Sorry, kiddo!"

Then the wave struck, the crest picking up the spinning globe and hurling it toward the tube mouth. It went through the plywood sheeting like a fist through a piece of paper.

Rick and Julia saw it coming. Rick had time to get his exit line in: "You crapped out, Kevin! *Snake Eyes!*"

The globe came thundering across the entryway, a steel-framed juggernaut. Dunne heard the crash and looked back over his shoulder just in time to see it coming.

Borne on a limb of furious black water, the globe disintegrated the double doors and smacked into Dunne, rolling on top of him, crushing him with all the fury of Jezebel.

The sea rushed into the tube, a black tide that rolled up equipment, dirt, and mud. Slightly ahead of it were Julia and Rick, running up the tube. It was like being in a subway tunnel, trying to outrace the train.

The globe got stuck in the tunnel, stemming the rush of water, the surge slowing as it was forced to go around and under the blockage.

Still, the sea lapped up the tunnel, distancing Julia and Rick, foaming around them up to their waists. It reached its farthest point of advance in the tube, then started to recede, sluicing back down the tunnel.

A piece of debris raced downward, knocking Julia's

feet out from under. She fell, wailing as she was sucked toward the jagged spiked globe at the end of the tunnel.

Rick lunged, grabbing hold of her ankle, being swept along downward with her. He flailed around underwater, grabbing at the walls of the tunnel, scrabbling for a handhold.

The backwash sucked them faster now, speeding toward the broken globe with its dagger-like outcroppings.

Rick was pulled underwater, his head banging on a handrail that stretched along one side of the tube. He twisted, kicking, beating at the rail, grabbing hold of it.

There was a wrench that felt like his arm pulling out of the socket, but he held his grip, now completely submerged. He held Julia's ankle, all that kept her from being flung into the globe's spiky shards.

Rick couldn't hold his breath any longer, but he couldn't get his head above water and still hold Julia. The current snaked and throbbed, trying to hurry her away.

He opened his eyes underwater, floating in a murky greenish-brown limbo eerily lit by the glow shining through the glass-ceilinged tunnel. It was absolutely silent, though he could feel, but not hear, the pounding of his heart.

He opened his mouth because he was out of air. Streamers of bubbles ripped from his mouth and nose. He couldn't breathe water, but that didn't stop him from trying.

He choked, his lungs filling with brackish slime. But he didn't let go, not of Julia or the handrail. He was a human rope being tugged to the breaking point at both ends.

I'm drowning, he thought. There was nothing peaceful about it, it hurt like hell.

But he didn't let go.

The water played out before he did. The receding wave lost its force, its speed, its level dropping as it drained out of the tunnel, dropping Julia and Rick on the mucky floor.

Julia sprawled on her hands and knees, gasping, coughing, spitting out water. She looked around for Rick and found him a short distance away. At first she thought he was dead, but then he moved, struggling in a semiconscious state.

She hooked her hands under his arms and dragged him uphill, fearful of another tidal onslaught. But the waves had crested at the high-water mark and lost much of their fierceness. They surged around the mouth of the tunnel, but advanced no more than half the distance they had advanced when the Big One had broken.

Julia only had the strength to drag Rick a couple of yards higher up the tube, but it was enough. They were safe from the water now.

She rolled him onto his back. His head turned to one side, slimy water running from his mouth and nose. She checked his mouth to make sure there were no obstructions to block his breathing, and began giving him mouth-to-mouth resuscitation, the Kiss of Life.

His chest heaved and he spasmed underneath her, his legs kicking. His eyelids fluttered and his eyes opened. He sat up, coughing and choking, spitting out water for a long time.

She lifted her shirt and reached around at the top of her pants for the envelope, but didn't find it. Then she reached inside her pants, and found it stuffed down there, waterlogged but safe. It would take more than a few hundred tons of seawater to damage those infrared photos.

Rick saw the envelope and nodded, smiling weakly, letting his head sink back wearily to rest against the tunnel wall. Julia sat beside him, putting her arms around him, holding him tightly.

That's how the cameraman found them later, when he and Anthea staggered out of their overturned truck, which had been toppled but not swamped by the wave.

They ducked into the tunnel mouth for shelter, and Julia heard them talking and called out for help. Then it was only a matter of time before the rescue party came.

The cameraman pointed the camera at Julia and Rick, recording the moment of posterity, while Anthea did the reporting—a real scoop for both of them.

TWENTY-TWO

Sound bites on the Road to Palookaville.

That's what Rick called them, those little videotaped moments in time that documented the meteoric rise-and-fall arc of his fifteen minutes of fame in the spotlight of the media circus, like snapshots in a family album, a family that came to a bad end: "Richard Santoro, Atlantic City's new police hero, received a special commendation from Mayor Frank Sanchini today for his role in . . ."

"Hero cop Richard Santoro took a well-deserved break from police work today with his son while the AirGuard investigation continues. . . ."

"Richard Santoro was unwilling to comment today on allegations of corruption that have been swirling around the police hero since Monday, when . . ."

"Richard Santoro was indefinitely suspended from police work today in the wake of . . ."

"Dirty cop? Richard Santoro may face criminal charges

for what investigators are calling a 'pattern of corruption' that dates back to . . ."

The next big media splash he'd get would probably be at his trial. He was in the shitter now, his life had turned to shit. Job gone, money gone, wife gone, girlfriend gone, kids gone, future gone—he was real gone.

It had all turned out just like Dunne had said it would. Poor Kevin. He had turned out to be a better prophet than a plotter. Would Dunne really have killed him? He'd always wonder.

Well, he was in Palookaville now, and he hadn't hit bottom yet. The Trident Motel was pretty far down the ladder, though. It was in Atlantic City and it was cheap, dirt cheap, like the furnishings, the neighborhood, and his fellow tenants.

When you get away from the Boardwalk, and you don't have to go too far, sometimes not more than a few blocks away from the shadows of the great gambling palaces, you're in a whole different world. Not a pretty one. Atlantic City can be a hard, tough town, as tough as they come.

His room was a dump and the hell of it was that he wouldn't be able to afford living there much longer, and when you can't make the weekly rent at the end-of-the-line outpost like the Trident, *then* where do you go?

Jail, probably, in his case. Definitely. At least he'd have a place to stay and three meals a day. That was a break.

Just when he thought things couldn't get any worse, a TV news crew popped up outside his doorstep. That's where they'd stay, since he was not letting them in, or even opening up the door to talk to them. His lawyer had given him a stern talking-to about keeping his mouth shut and not talking to reporters. It was wasted advice because Rick was so sick of the press that he hoped he'd never see another TV camera in his life. He wouldn't give anybody in the media the time of day. The lawyer had charged him for the advice anyway.

It had to be Lou. That sounded like a song lyric, but it was nothing but the truth, since the "reporter" encamped with the TV crew outside his motel-room door was none other than Lou Logan.

Lou was a big shot now, a celebrity "journalist," with an expensive suit and new hair. He was fronting for a News Channel 4 news team that had their cameras pointed at the locked door and curtained windows of Rick's seedy pad.

Lou banged on the door, shouting while the cameraman ran tape. "Rick? Come on, open up, it's me, Lou! I'm just trying to give you a chance to have your say! I want to tell your side, Ricky, you know how I feel about you!"

Yeah, that's why he wouldn't open the door.

"Rick? Ricky boy? Rick!"

Rick turned on the cheapo motel TV, turning the volume loud to a competing channel. He turned it up until he couldn't hear Lou any more. Finally, the TV crew went away.

That was in the morning. He stretched out on the bed in his undershirt and pants and took a nap. He did a lot of sleeping these days. It was free and it beat being awake.

He was awakened by the ringing phone. He was unsure what time it was at first—he felt more tired now than when he had gone to sleep. He threw his feet on the floor and sat up, rubbing his face with his hands. The

Goddamned phone wouldn't stop ringing until he picked it up.

Of course it wouldn't stop ringing, not when it was Angela, his soon-to-be-ex-wife, and she was boning him for more money.

"No, Angela, I didn't send it yet," he said, when she finally stopped for breath, allowing him to get a word in edgewise. Not the ones she wanted to hear, though.

"Because it woulda bounced, that's why," he explained. "I got suspension pay coming on Thursday. I'll send you that."

His wounds had healed but they still hurt, aching him constantly. He knuckled his eyes with a fist; they were tired and red-rimmed.

"Let me talk to Michael," he said. "Come on, he can be a few minutes late, just put him on, give me a break."

There was a pause, then he heard some back-and-forth on the other end of the phone, Angela telling his son to get on and talk and the boy saying he didn't want to, then he got on the line.

"Hi, Mikey, how ya doin'? Yeah? Ah, I'm okay. Whoa, whoa, wait a sec, will ya? Did you have practice last night? . . . Ah, I guess you better hurry then, huh? I love you, Michael. Give the phone back to—"

Click, buzz.

Michael had hung up. Rick held the phone to his ear until the dial tone cut off and a prerecorded voice came on telling him to please hang up the phone. It was the first time anybody had said "please" to him in a while, so he hung up.

He needed a smoke. Empty pack, no cigarettes.

"Figures," he said.

He lifted the edge of the curtain and looked outside.

He didn't see any news creeps staking out his motel-room door. He put on shoes and a shirt and took his keys and wallet from the night table. He checked his wallet. He had about enough left to buy a pack of smokes. Smoking was one of his last little pleasures left, but he'd have to scrimp on that, too.

Poverty was curing him of his bad habits.

He went out. It was late afternoon on a cool, gray day. The sky was slate gray, the sea was gray-green, and the sand was the color of ashes.

He walked along the Boardwalk, tearing the clear wrapper off a pack of cigarettes—an off brand, but at least it had nicotine in it. Only a handful of strollers were at the seaside, wandering the Boardwalk. There were plenty of people nearby, but they were all in the casinos. The casinos were always open.

Rick had had enough of people. He dreaded the thought that total strangers recognized him as that crooked cop they had seen on TV. An empty bench looked inviting and he sat down, his back to the sea, tapping the pack against his palm.

A sharp *crack* made him jump. He thought someone was shooting at him, then saw a bunch of construction workers on the Millennium's grounds, squaring away the details on a terraced garden pavilion. They wielded picks, hammers, and shovels. The sharp cracking sound came again, caused by a crew member wielding a sledgehammer on a concrete block.

The construction fence had come down some time ago, as the elaborate landscaping project neared completion. Work was proceeding at a brisk pace. A sign out in front said PARDON OUR DUST!

Corny bastards. Rick pulled out a cigarette and dug in his pocket for a lighter. A shadow fell across him.

"I brought you a present," Julia said. Bright, fresh, and clean, she stood over him, holding out a carton of cigarettes. His brand—when he could afford them.

Smiling, he took the carton, holding up the pack he had just bought. "When it rains, huh?"

"Mind if I sit down?" she asked.

He shoved over, and she sat down beside him. He offered her a cigarette, but she shook her head.

"That one I smoked with you was the only cigarette I've had in three years," she said.

"Oops."

"A reporter told me where to find you. I came twice before, but you were out."

"Yeah, I was out at the country club, trying to lower my golf handicap. I've had a lot of social engagements lately," he said.

"I'm surprised you stayed in town. I thought you'd want to move away."

"What, and leave my kingdom? Actually, I may be spending some time upstate."

"Upstate?" Maybe she remembered that Rahway State Prison was upstate, because she said, "Oh."

The breezes blew east, sending the cigarette smoke out to sea. After a while, Rick said, "I keep dreaming I'm back in that tunnel. Underwater. Only in my dream, I drown. From where I sit now, that looks like a good career move. I wonder what they woulda said about me then?"

She put a hand on his arm, her eyes warm, appealing. "You didn't have to do what you did. I know what it cost you. If it helps, I—"

"Don't try to make a hero out of me," he said too quickly, before she could finish whatever it was she was going to say. "If I hadn't put a face to you—if I hadn't liked your face—things might have gone a whole lot different."

"But they didn't."

He shrugged.

"I testified this morning. At the AirGuard hearings," she said.

"How'd it go?"

"Very well, I think. The whole system's been dumped and the company's being completely restructured. There are going to be a lot of indictments, all up and down the organization. The prosecutor said they even have a chance of implicating Powell himself."

"Fat chance," Rick said.

"Things have changed," Julia insisted. "You may not feel like admitting it right now, but you'll see. It's going to be different in Atlantic City."

His lips quirked in a meaningless smile. "You know, they say back two, three hundred years ago, pirates used to put phony lighthouses out near the big rocks in the bay. Right out there. Ships would set a course by the lights and crash on the rocks. Then everybody'd go out and rob 'em blind.

"Only one thing's changed around here since then. The lights are brighter."

He dropped his cigarette and ground it out underfoot. He looked at her. "So . . . Maybe someday I'll give you a call? You know—twelve to eighteen months from now."

"I'd like that," Julia said, smiling. He sure was a sucker for that smile.

203

He kissed her on the cheek, then started to pull away, but she pulled him back and kissed him on his cheek. He smiled, straightening up, stuffing the carton of cigarettes into the pocket of his army surplus coat.

"What the hell, at least I got to be on TV," he said. He turned and walked off, down the Boardwalk.

The gray cloud cover was thinning, and the sun was trying to break through. As he passed the awesome layout of the new casino hotel, he paused to watch as a giant crane lowered a cement pillar into place to one side of the yawning rocket-tail tubeway entrance fronting the Boardwalk. The pillar was shaped like a missile, having been cast by pouring concrete in an on-site casting mold, not far from the arena's loading docks.

Rick smoked a cigarette, watching the crane lower the pillar into its mounting with elephantine grace. When he looked back along the Boardwalk the way he had come, he saw that the wooden bench was empty—Julia was gone.

He went on his way. As he passed the pillar, his eyes were caught for an instant by a sunbeam breaking through the clouds and glinting on something bright and shiny embedded in the pillar's surface—something polished, green, and glinting.

Then the light changed and it was gone. Rick moved on, unaware that the glimmering green fleck of rare polished stone was part of a woman's ring, Serena's ring.

The Millennium would be built on human bodies and bones.